STILLWELL

A Haunting on Long Island

Michael Phillip Cash

NOV 2015

Disclaimer

The characters and events portrayed in this book are fictitious. Any resemblance to real persons, living or dead is coincidental and not intended by the author.

No part of this book may be reproduced, or stored in a retrieval system, or transmitted in any form or by any means, electronic, mechanical, photocopying, recording, or otherwise, without express written permission of the publisher.

Dedication

To my wife Sharon

"more than eternity"

Contents

Acknowledgments

Special thanks to my mom, whose love of history made this book possible.

Follow Michael on Twitter:
@michaelpcash
www.michaelphillipcash.com
If you find this book enjoyable, I really hope you'll leave a review on Amazon, Goodreads, and Barnes & Noble under *Stillwell*. If you have any questions or comments, please contact me directly at michaelphillipcash@gmail.com.

Other works by Michael Phillip Cash:

Brood X: A Firsthand Account of the Great Cicada Invasion

The Hanging Tree: A Novella

The Battle for Darracia Books I – II – III

The Flip

The After House

Witches Protection Program

Pokergeist

Coming Soon:

Monsterland

Prologue

Saturday

Paul turned from the dark window, twitching the drapes back in place. It was cold in the house; it had the dank feel of being unused. It had only been empty for a week, and yet it held a stale feeling of overripe food and decaying garbage.

The kids would be coming home tomorrow. He had sent them to his sister's place for the past week. It was too hard to have to worry about their schedules when he was sitting by Allison's side. The funeral was yesterday, and he asked his sister to keep them one more day. He needed to have some time to collect himself. He'd spent the last twenty-four hours sitting in the dark, staring at nothing, his mind too numb to think.

Lisa had taken over with the brisk efficiency of the nurse that she was trained to be. Stella was eating once again and Jesse and his twin, Veronica, were able to sleep at night. His sister's was the safe house, and while he desperately missed his children, he couldn't deal with their everyday drama while he stayed with Allison for her final weeks.

He played with the chain around his neck then placed the gold band that hung from it on his lips. He closed his eyes, feeling alone. It was his wife's wedding band and it had never left her finger from the time he had placed it there almost fifteen years ago.

Everything happened so fast. Too fast. His mind replayed the last six months in a montage of colors flashing like an out-of-control merry-go-round. Only it wasn't a happy ride. Well, he sighed, he had to admit that he did feel relief. It felt wrong to have this burden taken off his shoulders, but his wife didn't have to suffer anymore. He admitted to himself that he was weary too. She had gone from bad to worse in such a short time. She had slipped into a coma. He held her skeletal hand for a solid week, watching hope die alongside his wife. His family had brought in food, but he felt no hunger. As he stayed by her side, nothing seemed important. Paul stared at her face, memorizing every curve, her deep dimple, the mole she hated above her upper lip. Every second counted, and he wouldn't waste a minute on himself. His future yawned ahead in a great vastness of nothing that stretched endlessly before him. Alone, mute, and his thoughts jumbled in his head, he couldn't find words to say what he needed. Did she know how happy she had made him? Did Allison understand how much she meant to him? Could she know that his heart was so numb, he felt as though he were a corpse? Though he sat caressing her hand, could his wife sense the man next to her was spent, empty? It was that burnt-out feeling like after drinking so much that the liquor loses its taste and cigarettes burn with dying fire.

The irony was that he was the smoker, even though he had stopped when the twins were born, thirteen years ago. Allison wouldn't have it in the house. He cheated at work, chewing gum to disguise the smell on his breath. It had always been a huge fight, and while she painted all kinds of devastating scenarios if he continued to smoke, they never expected her to be the one to fall victim to cancer.

The twins were a rare handful for them. Married for just over a year, they were unprepared for the incessant work. He was building his reputation as a go-to guy for the McMansions that dotted Long Island's North Shore. The pull of work and two newborns tested their marriage. Allison breast-fed until utter exhaustion—or as he liked to call it "udder" exhaustion—made her stop. She always laughed at that.

Jesse, his son, was all brooding intensity, while Veronica, the elder twin by six minutes, was sweet, faithful, and resilient. They were golden children, kissed by sunlight, with blond hair, freckles, and odd silver eyes, like their mother. They communicated in a strange language that worked only for the two of them. A silent collusion between the twins created a special insight, and they knew exactly what the other was thinking. When words finally arrived, they could finish each other's sentences.

While he was happy with his family, Allison had wanted another child. Reluctantly, he agreed and was shocked at his devastation when she miscarried. His despair turned to relentless hope, and although they faced a period of secondary infertility, he pushed for seven years, and they became pregnant once again. He called her "Stella Luna," because she was the stars and moon to him.

With Stella, he had time to play. She was a fey child, filled with whimsy and a touch of an old soul.

Brown-haired and brown-eyed, she was the image of his older sister. Shut out of the twin's world, he made sure she never felt alone. When she turned two, her soulful brown eyes induced him to give up smoking once and for all. God, he wished he had a cigarette. Right now.

The house screamed with silence, its heavy pall smothering any sense of light. It closed over him. The acid ache in his gut he'd been experiencing since she got sick made its presence known. Padding to the kitchen, he went in search of milk to put out the fire. After he opened the refrigerator door, he stood for a minute staring at the empty shelves. He smelled the open carton of milk and recoiled at the odor. He never remembered buying it and could only guess how old it was. Well, the milk was plainly spoiled, as was the cheese. They had to be at least a month old. Maybe he should just eat the yogurt, let it kill him, and the kids would be done with mourning. Two for the price of one, he thought as he slammed the door. He'd have to go food shopping at some point. Yep, the kids were coming home tomorrow.

Paul slid on to the counter stool, holding his head in both hands. His skull ached as though there were a thousand hammers pounding behind his eyes. It pulsed with such intensity; he pressed his fingers against his eyeballs until all he saw was an iridescent halo. He sighed deeply and stretched backwards cracking his jaw as he yawned.

Dizziness assailed him and he gripped the granite counter with wet palms. "God," he thought, "am I going to faint?"

Sweat dotted his forehead and he shivered involuntarily as a gray mist enveloped him, chilling him to the bone.

Out of the corner of his eye, he sensed a shadow dancing around him. He felt paralyzed and couldn't move.

Suddenly nauseous, he rested his unstable forehead against the counter and said, "I gotta get some sleep."

CHAPTER ONE

Sunday

The early light of morning invaded the room, chasing the demons of darkness. Paul lay still, his eyes watching the shafts of sunlight piercing the holes of his shade. He didn't want to move, didn't want to get up. His bed felt safe. He rolled over, covering his head with the blanket, wanting to bury himself and pretend this day had never come. He couldn't believe his new reality.

It happened with the suddenness of a lightning strike. Life rolled by with the efficiency of the railroad, making milestones in everyday events. Then one day, they noticed a new pattern. There were headaches: premenstrual, postmenstrual, hormonal, and stress related. Oh, there was a sensible reason for all the signs leading up to the big kahuna. Numbness in her fingers—well, he told her she was exercising too much. Maybe it was that damn chiropractor she had started seeing. Carpal tunnel syndrome seemed like an easy excuse. They never thought of a brain tumor. Hah. She was thirty-four. Who got brain tumors at thirty-four?

Hopeful, they entered the cancer treatment center hand in hand, planning on battling this thing together. First came all the tests: CAT scans, PET scans, MRIs; every day there was a new test to see what the next step should be. Paul had never heard of any of these types of tests. He never thought it would become a part of his daily lexicon. He became adept at record keeping. The fancy leather-bound calendar the kids had presented to him for his birthday began to fill with appointment after appointment, and he became the one to keep everything straight. Allison had always run the show; he worked, and she was the planner. But she had retreated, shocked by the diagnosis. She curled inward, making him the point person. The ringmaster. Two-hour-long commutes to the best doctors in the city, waiting rooms filled with hopeful candidates, stories swapped of miracles, and science fiction-like treatments. Paul wrapped his boundless energy into keeping Allison's spirits up. Rallying her, he promised they would do whatever they had to do to overcome this obstacle.

It all seemed unreal to them when they got the first results. Mute with shock, they received the news in total disbelief. But the wormhole of cancer beckoned, sucking them in relentlessly. Now that he had lived in that universe, he knew the difference between a PET scan and a CAT scan. He could give a lecture on what to do if there was a fever or how to guard against infection.

Constipation became a conversation starter. Blood counts, iron deficiencies, and steroids—they were all part of his vocabulary. He learned about white blood cell counts and all the dangers that could incite a setback. He knew what Reiki could do or the power of music at a bedside. He spoke to anyone who could help them and shared his own information as well. His entire existence was dedicated to helping his wife in any way he could. Certainly surgery could have worked. He remembered grasping at straws. Root it out, cut it away, dangerous, of course, but with lasers a sure thing. Only minor lateral damage, the doctors thought, nothing they couldn't handle. But after a long twelve-hour day of surgery and waiting, it was still there on the next scan. A small dot, resistant. Chemo and radiation would handle that. It worked for that actress, yes, that one. She wore a head scarf at the Oscars. Hell, Michael Douglas had throat cancer, and a year later, was starring in movies again. He was making late night appearances on the talk show circuit while he was in treatment. See, cancer doesn't have to interrupt your life. If it worked for them, then it would work for Allison. Why not, she never even smoked.

Only it didn't work, and Paul and Allison and everyone who loved them fell into the rabbit hole of despair. They tumbled down, down, down where nothing makes anything feel better. How do you tell your mother you will not outlive her? How do you prepare your children? You won't be there for prom, graduations, or weddings? Lastly, how do you share with your partner, your best friend, that he will be alone for the rest of his life? Paul the husband and father had disappeared and he became a person running on autopilot, going from one hope to the next, trying anything for a cure, until he realized he had to change his tactics to be satisfied that he'd brought her an ounce of peace. He read every book to ease Allison's travail, but it was all for nothing.

Tears pooled in Paul's eyes, and he let them slide down in self-pity. His chest ached with hollow despair. He wanted to hold her. He needed her to stroke his head, like she did when she miscarried, and make him feel his misery was not alone. He missed her with every fiber of his being and didn't want to talk to anyone, anymore, ever again. He had never known a time without Allison; she was his better half. Alone, how was he going to live without her?

He became aware of noise first. The sun had sunk low over the rooftops, and he realized it was four in the afternoon, not four in the morning. He must have fallen asleep after all. Feet pounded on the steps and he heard all three of his kids scramble upstairs to his bedroom. They burst in and leaped on the bed. His sister Lisa stood with her arms crossed in the doorway. She was older than him by four years and short and stocky with a double chin she hated. They shared the same brown hair and dark chocolate eyes, but in some cosmic joke, he got the long lashes to go with it.

"I bought you groceries." She walked in and sat on the edge of the bed. She smiled gently. "I fed your monsters before we came, but they'll want snacks. Aunt Lou sent lasagna. It's in the freezer." Lisa resisted the urge to brush the tangle of hair from her brother's eyes. It was long and unkempt; there had been no time for him to take care of himself these last few weeks. His suit had hung on his large frame at the funeral. He looked abandoned and neglected, and she thought ruefully, he must have lost fifteen pounds. Looking down at the new spare tire decorating her waist, she mused that grief worked on people differently.

Veronica lay flat, her twin brother Jesse dangling off the edge of the other side of the king-sized bed. Paul assumed the lump under the covers was Stella.

"I have to be at work by six," she said. "Did you eat anything today? You gotta eat, Paulie." She looked at the wedding band on a chain, lying across his bare chest. She knew it was engraved on the outside but couldn't remember the words. On the inside, they both had their initials and the date of their wedding. Paul always joked that he'd never forget it that way. Yeah right, Lisa laughed to herself. Her brother worshipped his wife. Paul and Allison had the unique experience of love at first sight, if one could believe in that sort of thing. Added to that, it was when they were toddlers. She thought, how's that for fate? Well, look what fate did to them now. She looked at her brother's gaunt face and sighed. "Fate sucks."

"What?" Paul made a sour face. "What?"

Lisa stood. "Come on, I'll make you eggs." She was living proof that food made everything feel better.

He lay back down. "I'm not hungry."

As if it had a mind of its own, his stomach gurgled loudly and this set off the children with peals of laughter. It sounded strange in the house, and he fought the urge to yell at them to be quiet.

They didn't have to be quiet. No one was sick here anymore. They could be loud and silly, and he knew he had to get out of bed.

"Out, everybody out," he shouted playfully. "Give me five minutes. Would you mind making me coffee?"

Veronica jumped out of the bed, her silver eyes wide in her face, so like her mother's. His breath caught in his chest for a moment. "I'll make you coffee, Daddy," she offered. "Aunt Lisa showed me how to use the machine."

"Great." It came out gravelly; his voice sounded unused. "Yeah, that would be great."

The kids got up, and Stella poked her brown-haired head out of the covers. She slid onto the floor and picked up the dust ruffle to peer under the bed.

"What are you doing?" Jesse yanked her sloppy pigtail.

"Leave your sister alone," Lisa snapped.

"I heard something." Stella's wide brown eyes looked at them. "Didn't you hear it?" she asked again in a shocked whisper.

They all stood mutely looking at each other, and Jesse jumped onto the bed and screamed, "Stella's hearing things. Do you see dead people too?"

Paul grabbed his son and shook him hard. "Stop that."

Jesse's stubborn lip stuck out. He was angry; his resentment simmered under his freckled skin. He had Allison's fair skin.

Paul said, "Don't do that."

"Why? You gonna go back and hide under the covers?" his son snapped back.

Rage roiled in Paul and he held himself so rigid, he thought he might crack. A warm hand touched his muscled arm, soothing him. "Leave it, Paul. He's tired. The

6

kids have had a rough day. Jesse, apologize. Jesse," she hissed, "now!"

"Sorry," he mumbled, his eyes shiny with unshed tears. Paul pulled him close and ruffled his blond curls.

"Go get out some food and let's eat." He sighed as they filed out of the room, thinking how he was going to manage raising the children without his wife.

***

The kitchen smelled of eggs and cheese, and as much as Paul loved omelets, he had no appetite. They were all seated at the table. Ripped packages of snack foods, open containers of artificial dips, and brightly colored sugar candies were strewn all over the counter. At the very least, he thought, his newly planted wife would be rolling in her grave.

"Mom and Dad will stop by tomorrow. I told them you have to get into some kind of normalcy."

Veronica served him a hot cup of coffee. It had too much cream in it. He missed the way his wife always put in the right amount. His daughter was watching him expectantly as he took the first sip, scalding his tongue. "Ahhh," he said and smiled at her. "You made it just the way I like it." She returned a sunny smile, took Stella's hand, and went into the den. Then Lisa sat down next to him, her beefy hands closing up the open packages. Jesse retreated to the den as Paul heard the TV on and the muffled beginnings of a fight over the remote. Rolling his eyes, he started to rise, but Lisa put her hand over his, stopping him.

"You have to have a little patience. It's going to be hard. I know. You've got Mom and me. Dad will help too and then Allison's parents are going to want to come..."

She stopped when he gave her a martyred look. "Well, they are grieving too. At least once they go home to the Carolinas, you'll only have to deal with one set of parents. Look, I told everybody to lay off you guys. You have to find a rhythm. A new rhythm, you know."

Paul hung his head, the eggs tasteless in his mouth. He shoved the plate away.

"She's gone and you don't have the luxury to keep wallowing. Man up, Paulie..." She gestured to the den. "You don't have time to be the grieving widower. The kids need you."

"Thank you, Dr. Phil," Paul replied. "I don't want to do this."

"Well, you don't have a choice." She started cleaning up the mess. "When do you have to go back to work?"

"Soon. They give three days. I've been out so many. They've really been amazing, but I can't afford to take much more."

"Set up a routine. The kids need it. Jesse's been a horror. Stella's barely talking and Roni's like a shadow. If you don't start acting more normal, the kids are going to lose it."

"I don't want to be normal," Paul insisted. "I want to go to sleep and wake up and find everything back like it was."

"Well," Lisa told him from the sink where she was washing the dishes, "we don't always get what we want."

***

He managed to get the kids ready for bed. Jesse closed the door in his face asking for privacy. Veronica kissed him good night. As he helped braid her blonde locks, his heart twisted. They were the same color as Allison's. She was using her mother's brush, and when she asked him to help her get out the tangles, he saw his wife's hair entwined with his daughter's, trapped in the tines of the steel brush.

His throat closed up, clogged with emotion, and although he said good night, he found he couldn't say anything else.

Stella's room felt ice cold. It was mid-September and unseasonably cool. He checked the window and found it closed, but a draft blew from a vent. He flipped the switch shut, watching her curtains stop fluttering to settle against the windowsill.

"Oh, I thought that was Mommy's ghost."

"There's no such thing as ghosts, Stella Luna." He sat on the bed.

"How do you know? Maybe Mommy's a ghost."

Paul lay down next to her on the bed and wrapped his arms around her. Stella reached in and took out the chain around his neck. She put Allison's ring on her pointer finger, her eyes downcast. He loved the way her lashes feathered against her plump cheeks.

"Mommy is safe in Heaven." He breathed in her sweet baby smell. Lisa must have given her a bath.

"No, she's not. She's here," Stella insisted. "Well, she was at Aunt Lisa's and now she's here."

"If it makes you feel better to think she's…"

"No, Daddy," Stella said even more seriously. She looked at him without blinking. "She's here. I heard her."

He gently disengaged her hands from the chain and started to rise. "OK baby doll, lay down," he said then kissed her head. "She's here."

Stella smiled, satisfied, and watched her father leave the room, the door slightly ajar. He heard her whisper, "You can come out now, Mommy. He left."

Lisa left hours before. The house felt empty. Shutting all the lights, he walked from room to room, picking up discarded clothes and leaving them in the laundry room. They had hired a cleaning woman toward the end—someone to keep up on the housework as Allison's body failed. He'd have to see if he could strike a deal to get her a few times a week. It was going to be hard, with all the bills; he'd missed so much work and hadn't sold a house in a while. He shuddered thinking he'd have to start showing houses again. He worked a few miles from his home. He loved this neighborhood. Settled by the English in the 1600s, it was rich in history. Both Paul and Allison had grown up here, next door to each other. They had played as babies together; their mothers had a great friendship that went back to when they had each bought the first new tract homes and developed them into a model neighborhood in the seventies. Paul was a year and a half older, but they had a lifetime of block parties, carnivals, and barbeques that they had shared. There was no question that they were meant for each other, and when they married, they purchased a home in the newer section of the town. A colonial built in the 1980s. It was a bit cramped. They never expected to have three children when they bought the house. They were planning a move to the next village of Jericho, but then Allison got sick. He was a broker in one of the more prestigious Long Island realty companies. A boy wonder, he surfed the housing boom and made tons of money. He had a stellar reputation for finding the right match, and young couples loved working with him. He was best known for nailing great deals that worked within a budget which made him extremely sought after. The added bonus was that Allison could quit her job as a buyer in the city and stay home to raise their growing family. He'd had the perfect life, the perfect wife. Now, to say the least, not so much. He needed a big sale to catch up on all the income he had lost. She had gotten sick in early April. The year before the illness invaded his home, the housing market had tanked, so they had been living off their savings for some time. He lost the whole end of the spring season, making a fraction of what he should have. Luckily, his partner Molly had been able to score some small sales, but he was the strongest of his team. The whole summer he barely left his ailing wife's side. She entered hospice in late August and was gone the second week of September. The funeral was two days ago, and he hadn't done any work in almost four weeks. He didn't even know what was out there.

He meandered to the makeshift office he created for himself in a corner of the finished basement. It allowed him to search for listings and even check out Facebook once in a while to see what his college buddies were up to. The kids generally played in their rooms, so it was nice to get some private time. But he hadn't really sat at his home office desk in just over six months. Everything concerning Allison and her treatments filled his days, so for a few minutes, he felt rootless. It was strange to turn on his computer to read things that didn't revolve around sickness. He opened his laptop, and a bright picture of Allison displayed on the screen. A smile tugged at his lips. It felt rusty, like an unused thing. They took that picture when the kids were playing at a friend's house. Horsing around in the bedroom, he took revealing pictures of her chest that she had made him erase. He was playing with a new phone he had bought and wanted to test it out. Allison dared him to upload one of the less risqué pictures to his computer to save it as a background. She got sick about three weeks after the picture was taken. A thick cloud of sun-kissed locks framed her face, her lips swollen from the wild make-out session they'd shared. She had the contented look of a well-loved woman, and that she was. He had made long, slow love, knowing they had very little time before the kids returned. He didn't care, and when she balked that the children would be arriving soon, he teased her by doing the things she loved, all the while telling her they had all the time in the world. He had no idea how time was running out for them. He didn't realize that lazy afternoons with perfect loving would one day be a memory. He stared at her beautiful face and couldn't help but wonder if the cancer was brewing in this picture. She looked healthy; she had even gained a little bit of weight. Her effervescent smile lit up the whole screen. The beacon of her warmth reached out from the picture. She had the capacity to light up a room with her laughter. Everyone liked her; she was the type of person that never spoke negatively about others. If she didn't have something nice to say, it went unsaid. He touched the tiny mole on her upper lip on the screen, sighing, missing her company. "Shit," he said. "We didn't have enough time after all."

He didn't remember how long he sat staring at the desktop picture. Snapping out of his stare, he scrolled through the new listings his office had taken on. There were quite a few exclusives, houses that should have been his. Calls he had made to older couples looking to downsize, that he never followed up on. He had no inventory himself, since the market had crashed. He stopped soliciting new listings. He'd have to get back out there, that was for sure.

There were thousands of emails, most of them advertisements for products he had purchased for Allison's treatment. Goji juice, blueberry the natural antioxidant, invitations to test studies, just in case the one she was participating in had halted. His hand hovered over the delete button. Pausing, he decided to go through them. He had a few leads, people looking to rent, which was always good. Referrals from other happy clients, two or three emails each, that had moved on to someone else when he failed to return an answer. A few estates, people he knew trying to sell houses belonging to relatives that had passed away. One caught his eye. It was a returning client. An old friend, sort of. He had gone to school with both Melissa and her husband, Craig Andrews. They all ran in the same crowd when they were younger. He never really liked Melissa, but Craig had been a good friend. Allison never said anything, but he knew she didn't like her. They did go to dinner a couple times a year, and he always had to coerce his wife into attending. He knew that Melissa made Allison uncomfortable, and he didn't blame her; she was a phony and he knew it. Melissa had asked him to sell her parents' home after they both died. Now it seemed her husband's parents had passed away. He had known them pretty well and was surprised that both were gone. He didn't remember hearing that either was sick, but he had been out of the loop for some time. They had one of the biggest and more famous mansions in the area. She wanted to unload their house. The email was two weeks old. He picked up the phone and cursed. She probably went with someone else.

He punched in her number. "Hi, Melissa."

"Paul? How are you doing?" she asked hesitantly. "I heard about Allison. Is she doing better?"

"Well…" Paul sighed, his throat was thick. He hated to have to keep repeating it. It never got easy. "She passed away last Friday."

"Oh Paul, I am so sorry. How are you…and those kids? Oh my, how are the kids doing?"

He cleared his throat, swallowing the lump lodged there. "It's been hard, but you know…"

"Yes. I know. I've been waiting for you to call. We would have gone to the funeral. What happened?"

"It was fast; just over six months ago, she was diagnosed. She wanted to keep everything normal." He laughed sadly. "As if anything can be normal with brain cancer. She didn't want a fuss and asked for immediate family only at the service. I had to honor her wishes. The kids stayed with my sister 'til today. I'm trying to get back on track."

"She was a great person. I didn't really know her well, but she was always so sweet and helpful." It sounded like she took a long drag on a cigarette. "We waited for you, Paul. I wouldn't dream of going with anyone else. You're the best in the area."

With this Paul felt a lead weight come off his chest.

"You did such a good job on my parents' house. Even in this economy, you got us more than we expected. This house is not going to be an easy sell."

"Nothing is an easy sell in this market," he added.

"It's not that. You may not want to take it. You didn't know?"

"Know what?"

"The house. It was a murder-suicide. Craig's father killed his mom and then shot himself."

"Jeez. Melissa, I am so sorry. I didn't know. How horrible."

"It was devastating. No motive. Well, not that we know of, and the mess. I hired two teams to clean it up."

15

A chill danced along his spine, and he fought the images of Craig's parents. They were polite people, very proper. A bit on the cold side, but they had always treated him nicely. As a teenager, it was *the* place to be. He had swum in their pool many times during the hot summers as well as attended quite a few parties in the pool house. The amenities were unbelievable, and he had crashed regularly there throughout high school with the rest of the crowd. For a very short time, he and Craig had a garage band that practiced a couple of times a week. Surrounded by acres of undeveloped land, they could be as loud as they liked. With no small amount of pride, they won second place at the High School Battle of the Bands. This got them a few gigs in local bars, but to the relief of all parents concerned, it fizzled out when they all left for college. The Andrews family was very rich, since it had been here for eons, part of the original colonists to settle in the States. The family members were a permanent part of the landscape; he remembered reading one of them was an important senator in the past.

"How are Craig and his brothers handling it?" Craig had two brothers and a sister. It was a large family and he knew the siblings had all moved out of New York when they completed their education.

"Warped, as usual. I don't know about men and the way they don't acknowledge grief—" she stopped suddenly realizing to whom she was speaking. "They had a private funeral. There's not much to say after murder involving your mother and father. Scott and Roy went back to Palm Springs and left us with the mess. Ellen—you remember her, Craig's sister—is busy saving whales in Alaska and never bothered coming in." She sighed again. "Craig left for Asia the next day. One of the factories had a fire. Lucky me," she said and laughed without humor.

Paul shrugged and realized she couldn't see his movements. Wanting to get off the phone, he said, "I'll call him tomorrow. What was the name of the house again, Stillwater?"

"Stillwell," she said coldly.

"Oh right, Stillwell. Hey, is that wishing well still on the property? We used to throw coins down there as kids."

"Yes, nothing's changed." Melissa was getting bored.

"Do you have the keys?"

"I have the rotary luncheon tomorrow, so let's say we'll meet there Tuesday at 10:00 a.m. Are you up to it? Craig gets home from China tomorrow. He's been away for almost two weeks. I've had to handle everything myself. The fucking bodies were being lowered into the ground and he was already on his way to the airport, along with the rest of his useless family. The father's brothers stayed. You remember, his uncles. I wish they'd leave."

"He has two, right? One of them built the senior housing on Cobble Hill."

"Yeah, he's a contractor and is bothering me to give him the house. He's coveting the forty acres Stillwell sits on. He wants to put up another one of those fifty-five and older communities. I'm not letting that happen. He screwed us over with Craig's grandparents' inheritance. He took a piece of land we were supposed to get. I'll give the house away before I see him get anything out of it."

"Doesn't the house belong to the whole family?"

"No, Craig's father inherited it from the grandparents. Each of the brothers got a piece of land. They are only entitled to some of the contents. We'll see about that, though."

"What about the other brother?"

"He's a lawyer. Selfish prick. He just wants his share of the pie. They are like a pack of hyenas...his uncles."

It was quiet for a minute. "I just want to dump the house," she continued. "It has bad vibes."

"Do you have a number in mind?" Paul asked.

"Craig mentioned the land alone is worth twenty-three million. I know the market is soft."

He paused. "It depends on how fast you want it to go. Most people are going to rip down the house either way. I have to look at my comps, but I'm thinking if you want a quick sale, nineteen million will get a lot of notice."

"It's low, and I have to ask Craig. I'll let you know Tuesday, after I speak to him."

There was an awkward silence on the phone. Selling Stillwell for nineteen million would repair Paul's losses for all of this year. He needed this listing.

"I'm sorry about your in-laws, Melissa," he said, breaking the silence. "They were lovely people. I remember going to the house on prom night...They threw us a party. It was the biggest house in Locust Valley."

"And the oldest. It's been there for over a hundred years."

"Do you have any of the history on it? Anything I could use to get rid of the taint of their deaths?"

"No, I hate the place. Always have."

"I'll go to the library and see what I can dig up about the house. Thanks, Melissa. I really mean it. I have been wallowing for the last week. I couldn't get out of bed. I have to thank you. You probably saved my life."

"No problem, Paul. What are friends for? You need anything?"

"I'm good."

"See you the day after tomorrow," she replied.

Paul hung up the phone. He closed his computer files to see Allison's picture again. He stared at it.

"Good night, Ally."

He shut the laptop and walked back upstairs. He wandered into the den then reached for the remote while falling onto the couch. It was the first time he turned on the TV in over a month. He looked over at where Allison used to sit and knew he would be watching television alone.

Flipping the channels, he settled on a travel show and actually got involved in the commentary of the third-world country the host was visiting. A chill swept through the room rattling the blinds on the window. Goose bumps danced up his arm, so he took a blue, knitted afghan his aunt had made and wrapped it around his torso. As he rested his head on a pillow, he observed the man on television eat the innards of rodents. His mind shut down, his eyes did all the work, and he drifted as he watched. Strategies of selling a house of historical significance flitted through his mind. Photographers, brochures, a massive open house, he mentally checked off the coming responsibilities. The realtor in him perked up. For the first time in a very long time, Paul found something to be interested in. He wondered if he should call his sister and let her know.

CHAPTER TWO

Monday

The next morning, Paul woke, still on the couch, the sound of his kids stirring filling the room. Veronica and Jesse were embroiled in an all-out fight by the bathroom. His son was banging on the door trying to evict his twin.

Paul sensed his son's anger and went upstairs to check out the scene. He put his hand on Jesse's wiry shoulder. "Go to my bathroom."

"No, make her get out." Jesse's face was crimson, his eyes shiny with anger and frustration.

Stella popped her head out. She was half dressed, wearing what appeared to be purple pants with a bright red shirt. Multicolored socks covered her feet. She looked like a circus character.

"Stella, you can't wear that. Go change."

"Why? I like it," she insisted.

Jesse started kicking the bathroom door with venom.

"Stop!" Paul shouted, losing patience.

"You always favor the girls. You always go easy on them. I hate you!" He ran to his bedroom, slamming the door.

Paul followed him, his own anger boiling over. "Go to my bathroom."

"He won't," Stella said softly, following him and trailing her striped socks behind her. "He said Mommy is in there. He's scared."

"Stop, Stella. Mommy is not in there." He bent down and held her by the shoulders, and with his eyes soft, he said, "You have to stop saying that. Tell Roni to hurry."

"She's not doing anything in there. She just wanted to make Jesse crazy."

Jesse was having an epic meltdown, Veronica was hiding in the bathroom, and Stella was dressing like a transvestite. He didn't know where to start or what to do. This was Allison's job. He brought home the bacon. She handled all this. He came home, and they would be sitting anesthetized by TV or buried in homework. This was her territory. In his line of work, he was usually showing houses all weekend, so she took the kids to everything. She knew their friends, did the playdates, took them to petting zoos. The only time he went on outings with them was when long weekends interrupted sales or during a slow spell, usually midwinter, when looking for homes died down. They vacationed hard, though, he thought with a smile, remembering those trips to the Caribbean or cruises where they crammed two weeks of activities into five days.

The phone rang and Paul shouted, "Veronica, get the phone!"

He heard a muffled shout, "I'm in the bathroom. I can't."

Stella ran for the kitchen. "I'll get it."

Paul shrugged and knocked on Jesse's door. "Jess, open up."

"Go away."

"I'm not going away. Open up," he said more seriously now. There was a long pause. "I'm gonna count to three."

"Dad, I'm not five anymore!"

"OK, one, two..."

"It's Nonni!" he heard Stella shout. "She wants to know—"

"Not now." Paul shouted back. The door opened a crack, "What's up, Jesse?"

Jesse sat on the edge of his bed. He was a skater and loved the whole Tony Hawk scene. He had on skinny jeans with a plaid button-down. His blond hair lay lank over his eyes.

"She knows I have to get ready too. Mom would have had her out of there. Veronica always wants to hog the bathroom. Then if Stella gets in, forget it."

"Use mine."

"No." His son's lower lip trembled.

"Why? We'll call it the boys' room. You and I can share."

His son's face was a study in misery. "I can't," he whispered. Paul waited. "Her perfume. The room smells like

Mom. I don't want to go in there." His thirteen-year-old voice cracked and almost disappeared.

"I miss her too." Paul looked bleak. "I'll speak to Roni."

He left and entered the kitchen. Stella was sitting on the counter chatting with his mother, twining the telephone cord around her small fingers. Her brown hair was in a sloppy side ponytail. He'd have to fix that before she left for school.

"It's Nonni," she said then smiled up at him. Bouncing her legs back and forth, she looked like a forest sprite. Her small, triangular face beamed as she spoke to her grandmother.

When he stared blankly back at her, she said slowly as if he were an idiot, "On the phone, Daddy. It's Nonni; she's checking up on you."

He kissed her upturned nose, admiring her elf-like face. He then took the phone and made short work of his conversation with his mother.

"I don't have time, Ma. No, we're fine. He's OK. Adjusting." There was a period of silence, and Paul didn't know if he could talk even if he wanted, so he nodded mutely. He was miserable. "Got it. I know. If I need you, I'll call. Right. Love you too."

Breakfast was another disaster. They didn't have the right cereal. Didn't he know that Stella couldn't tolerate whole wheat? He pulled her hair when he brushed it. Mommy never did that. Roni had a bad taste in her mouth and wasn't hungry, and Jesse stared at the waffle as if he had never seen one.

Exasperated, he demanded, "Tell me what would make you happy?"

Since they all knew that there was nothing in this world that would alleviate their pain, Paul thought later it was a decidedly dumb question.

One by one, the kids kissed him good-bye. Paul was relieved that they went back to school. It would be healthy for them, he thought. They could talk about other things like Twitter, Angry Birds, and whatever else kids talk about these days.

He called the housekeeper, Mirabelle, to set up a new schedule. He was a shrewd negotiator with everyone but his maid. If she wasn't cleaning the right way, he would just tell Allison, but now there was no buffer. He had to step up and tell Mirabelle exactly what he needed. She would come three times a week. Could she cut him slack on the price? She was very sorry, but her time was money, and if she was going to take care of his hellhounds and add food shopping and laundry to her load, someone was going to have to pay for it. Paul wasn't in the mood to haggle with someone who spoke broken English. But when it came to talking money, she somehow understood everything. He would just have to make the numbers work. He needed to get out there and sell something. He locked the house and forgot to put on the alarm then had to return. Satisfied, he also took out the garbage and headed to his office.

***

His commute was only minutes, but it seemed strange to be heading to work. It had a foreign feeling, like he hadn't been there in ages. As he put on the radio in his car, he twisted the dial, looking for his station. For some reason it wouldn't catch a signal. At the light he searched, stopping where the static seemed to die down. There was a garbled voice repeating what seemed like a mantra. Raising the volume, he leaned forward. It was unbelievable. The harsh noise caused a shiver to race up Paul's spine. It continuously repeated, "She's mine, she's mine, she's mine…" Paul flipped the radio off, sitting rigid until a horn honked impatiently. He missed the light, causing a minor backup. Pressing the gas, he made a hard left and tentatively turned the radio on again, but the station was gone. In its place was the clear voice of a radio announcer talking about the ballgame. Shrugging, he pulled into the parking lot at work. He looked for his name on a metal sign identifying his spot but noticed they had placed him in the rear and put a new boy wonder, the nephew of the current owners, in the parking space up front. Well, that's not promising, he thought to himself as he took his briefcase and walked into the building. He stepped in gum and cursed loudly as it held fast to his shoe. His ankle twisted, but the shoe was stuck to the pavement. He bent over and removed the loafer, swore once again, and scraped the sticky, pink gum from the sole of his shoe. "I needed this," he muttered under his breath. His shoe continued to stick to the ground and he wondered if it was a sign that he should have stayed home today.

The door had an old bell that tinkled when he opened it that made him feel foolish, as if it was announcing his return. He sensed all the faces of his colleagues turn to look at him as he walked past their cubicles, their sympathetic smiles making his insides turn to ice. Allison and he had agreed not to make a grand funeral. His wife had been specific that she didn't want anything dragged out for either him or the children. "Normal," she told him. "I want life to be normal as soon as possible." She stroked his arm as she told him, "You'll see, you will need to get back to living as soon as possible."

As if, he thought bitterly. He wanted to sneak into the room so he ducked his head, not wanting to hear the condolences that ripped the pain anew. He nodded, without making eye contact, heading straight for his cubicle.

It was in an old building, one of the pre-Revolutionary War cottages that dotted the island. It had a faint woodsmoke smell and was always damp. Paul put in many hours there, searching out leads. Up until Allison got sick, he was the most prolific agent. He had pulled back a bit and now had to reestablish himself. New plants decorated the front entryway. Had he been gone that long? Everything to him was a blur.

Molly was there; she was a senior agent and his selling partner. In fact, she had trained him. She sat cross legged at her desk, her bohemian-style dress floating around her ample form. "Oh Paul, hon. I was so sad to hear about Ally." She got up and waddled over. "I have missed you so much." She wore colorful shoes that never quite matched her outfits.

Paul winced but let her hug him. She was harmless, a sweet person, a bit ditsy, but good company overall. She belonged in Malibu, not Oyster Bay, but her father owned a casting agency for commercials in Lindenhurst so she stayed on Long Island, never getting married. On weekends she and her father would hit every casino in the Northeast just because they could. Everything about her was big: her hair, her dresses, her boobs, oversized sweaters, but most of all, her heart. He truly liked her. They had great chemistry and an easy partnership. They had worked together for years. She was good with rentals, and he made the monster sales that fed them both. She couldn't survive without him. He appealed to the new kids coming in looking for homes better than Molly's hippy, dippy ways.

"It wasn't long. She only suffered at the very end."

"I don't want to talk about it." She raised a hand that sported one-inch-long cherry red nails that reminded him of fangs. She teased her hair a bit. "I want to remember your wife in all her glory. She was a beautiful girl. Sweet. It's a shame." Her blue eyes welled.

Paul's office was a mess. Papers piled so high he couldn't see his desktop. The last time he was here, Allison was alive and in treatment. He remembered leaving work thinking everything was going to be OK. They just had to get through this next round of radiation or chemo. Bleakly, he moved one pile of paper to the other side of his desk and then back again. He didn't know where to start. A few of the other agents wandered by, and he had to relive that conversation about fourteen times. Yes, it was a blessing. Yeah, the kids are sad. Such a terrible thing to happen to one so young. How many times would he have to let others feel better, so that they could be socially correct and stab him in the heart. "It's enough!" he wanted to shout. "I don't want to talk about it anymore. IT HURTS!" He longed to stand on his desk and scream. Eyeing his stack of memos, he couldn't concentrate on anything. He glanced at his wristwatch, a Breitling, Allison's tenth anniversary present to him; he noted the time. She always called him about now. They would discuss dinner, plans for the kids, sweet, stupid stuff that they always shared. He thought back to careless conversations where he barely listened because he was busy. How dare he not have time for her? Why did he squander minutes they might have shared? How stupidly wasteful was he? He never realized there was going to be a limit. Well, that call wasn't going to be coming today. He'd have to think about feeding the kids later. He stared angrily at a family picture taken last summer. They had gone to Martha's Vineyard and had a volcanic fight. Allison wanted to spend the day with the kids, and he insisted they go to a client who invited them to his vacation home. Allison begged for family time. The business had taken over his life and he had hardly any time for them. The entire week dissolved into a tense showdown filled with pregnant silences. He wished he could go back and fix their last carefree days together. He didn't know it was going to be their final one as a family.

"Harrison's trying to steal your thunder. I have a bunch of leads. I've been saving them for you." Molly looked around. "You have to catch up. You need a couple big sales. You don't want them giving your desk away."

"What, Molly. Do you know something? I noticed they stuck me in the rear of the parking lot." Stopping what he was doing, he turned to look her in the eye. He needed his job, now more than ever.

Molly shrugged then glanced around to make sure nobody could hear them. "Fanny's nephew is chomping at the bit to get your contacts. You have to step it up. I know this business. It's dog eat dog. They won't waste space on someone not pulling in numbers." She put a stack of pictures of homes with scribbled phone numbers on his desk. "Just sit there and call. I heard Melissa Andrews has been looking for you." She rolled her eyes. "That'll be a catch if you can nail that. She wants to sell her in-laws' place. Messy business. Even if the commission is huge, I don't like this sort of sale. Hard to sell a murder house. I could never do it alone. The Thompson one sat for over two years until some Texans bought it. They weren't afraid of the ghosts."

"Don't start that stuff with me, Molly. I have enough with Stella."

She rolled right next to him and whispered, "What? Has Stella seen something? You must tell me."

"Nothing. Imagination. I don't want to talk about it. I gotta get to work."

He worked right through lunch, cold calling, every so often a frigid pit of hopelessness settled in his stomach. Acid jumped to the back of his throat reminding him to take antacids. This was a new thing. He had never suffered from indigestion. Allison's illness had brought him a lasting present, chronic acid reflux. Standing, he tried to relieve the pressure under his breastbone. The back of his throat burned, and he chomped on Tums like they were candy. He knew that he was speaking to people, wrote their info, but as soon as he hung up the receiver, he couldn't remember what he had said. He looked at his computer screen, knowing nothing was registering. It was like the grief hung over him as a constant reminder. His chest hurt with the ache of a lifetime. He remembered when they lowered the casket. His heart had shattered, breaking into tiny shards of glass, and a great emptiness enveloped him. Every time he envisioned the mental picture of her last days, he clenched his eyes shut, opening them gradually, hoping nobody else saw his agony. He didn't know how long he sat there, staring at nothing.

His work phone lit up and he read his sister's name on the computer screen.

"Hi, Lee, what's up?"

"What the hell, Paul! Is your cell on?"

He looked all over his desk and couldn't find it. Reaching behind, he felt it in his jacket pocket. "I must have forgot to turn it on this morning."

"Dad and Mom are going nuts. They've been trying to reach you. The school called them because they couldn't get you. Jesse's in the principal's office."

"Shit."

"You have to go. I have to make up hours. I'm sorry, but I can't go for you. Mom and Dad had to go for the consult on the cataract surgery. They've put it off too long."

"I know," he said as he slipped on his jacket. "I'm sorry. I'll go get him."

***

The middle school was in the next town. Just next to the high school, it was ranked number two in the nation for education behind some school in Westchester. The standards were high, especially since 99 percent of the kids that graduated went to college. The teachers and faculty meant business.

After a lengthy talk with the dean, he went into the principal's office. While Jesse sat sullenly outside, they decided that he had to finish the day.

"We are so terribly sorry about Mrs. Russo. She was a wonderful lady," the principal said. She was very professional, her salt-and-pepper hair in a neat bob. She had on thick, trendy glasses that were oddly smudged with grease.

Paul cleared his throat but couldn't take his fascinated gaze off the incongruous, filthy eyeglasses. How could she look so professional and incompetent at the same time? He resisted the urge to grab the glasses and wipe them on the tail of his shirt. She spoke, but all he focused on was the cloudy lenses.

"It is natural for Jesse to be acting out, but he was too disruptive in class and his English teacher asked for us to deal with him."

"What? Oh yes, I understand. I will talk to him tonight."

"Mr. Russo…" She paused leaning forward. Paul recoiled automatically, moving backward still caught in the cloudy stare. "We'd like to suggest grief counseling for the twins."

Heat rose from his neck to his face. It was hard enough dealing with the kids, but now the system wanted them to see a shrink. "I don't know. I don't think so."

"A grief counselor will help them cope," she told him gently. She wrote down a number on a piece of paper and handed it to him. "Stacey Friedman has done a great job with many of the children in our community who have suffered losses. Make an appointment, Mr. Russo. It will do them a world of good."

"The kids' mom died last week. They need time. It's barely a week," he repeated. This woman clearly couldn't see straight out of her lenses. "I need time to see what the best thing is for them." He thought about Allison, her love, her strength. "I will help them cope."

"I have a note here from Veronica's social studies and gym teachers. Naturally, we understand they were going through a terrible ordeal with the illness, but now that... well, you understand, the children's mental health is our utmost concern."

Paul didn't want to fight the principal. This was only the second time he was meeting her. The other time he was out one night at a local steakhouse with Allison and she was there dining with her significant other. Allison introduced them and he didn't remember her first name. Aside from that, if she didn't know the difference between clean and dirty spectacles, what made her such an expert on his children?

"I will see to it this week," he responded. He had a strong family that never reached out for help. Always close, they had weathered many storms together. His parents, Allison's parents were rocks. Even-keeled. How would he explain this to them? Would they think he was not up to helping his own children? Psychology was not in their DNA. Another problem landed squarely on his shoulders, weighing them down.

On the way out, he crouched and touched his son's chin, pushing him to make eye contact. "You OK?"

"Great." Jesse looked away.

"What do you want me to do?" Paul asked him.

"You can't do anything. Are we done?"

"They said you can go back to class. I'll see you at four."

Jesse walked away without a reply, leaving Paul standing alone in the empty hallway.

***

It was just before two, and Paul knew he had to be home for Stella's bus. There was no time to stop at the library, so he swung the car onto Route 25A and headed for the Stillwell estate. Route 25A was a state highway on Long Island. It served as the main east-west route for most of the North Shore, running for seventy-three miles from the Midtown Tunnel to Calverton in Suffolk County.

The route was known for its scenic path through decidedly lesser-developed areas such as Brookville, Fort Salonga, Centerport, and the Roslyn Viaduct. It was known by various names along its routing, the most prominent of which included Northern Boulevard.

He wanted to walk the grounds before he met with Melissa tomorrow. He felt outside his body, as if he was moving in slow motion. He knew that he drove but didn't feel the passage of time. Still on autopilot, he was in a strange, suspended kind of state where things happened by rote. They got done, but he just couldn't recall how. He reached out to the seat next to him and caressed the worn leather. It was Allison's seat. His soul mate. She would know what to do with Jesse. His hand met empty air and closed into a tight fist. "Get your shit together, Paul," he told himself. Hesitantly, he turned on the radio and felt a sense of relief when he heard Elton John singing "Yellow Brick Road."

He pulled into the overgrown driveway surrounded by tall pine trees, just off the main road. Huge old gates that had rusted over years ago and were left open guarded Stillwell. Paul remembered they never closed them; they were broken at a wild party in the last century, by ancestors of the current owners that lived in the house. He had researched today on the Internet, learning the house was built by a prosperous farmer during the 1700s. This landowner was the first Andrews to arrive here from England. Craig had an attic filled with clothing belonging to different eras. Paul loved a Revolutionary War drum they had found there. Craig had made a wedding present of it and gave it to Paul and Allison when they married. He treasured it, and although it was buried under paper in his office, he liked to clean it off and bang on it with the children.

The house had a sorrowful reputation. Nothing tangible, just an overall aura of sadness that was often the subject of newspaper articles. He couldn't recall any of the stories, only that there was something sad associated with the house. As if that wasn't enough, now it could add a murder-suicide to its history, just for atmosphere, he thought ruefully.

At the end of a two-mile gravel driveway, the house stood proudly, surrounded by ancient trees that were lush with the beginning of fall colors. It was a two-story colonial, seventeen bedrooms, he recalled, and with seven or eight bathrooms. Maybe more. There were parts of the house he had never seen. There was a ballroom and a servants' wing. It was locked up. A lone band of ripped yellow police tape floated on the crisp early fall air; it was attached to one of the wrought-iron railings. The word "caution" on the police tape waved in the breeze as if beckoning him to enter. He had no key, so he parked the car on the top of the gravel driveway and walked through the dense overgrowth toward the back terrace. He'd have to tell Melissa to have a gardener clean it up. It was silent there. He couldn't hear any traffic from the main road, only the gentle chirping of birds and the trees swaying. There was a wall of French doors. It was beautiful. He knew the ballroom was here. A lone dove called gently for her mate, breaking the silence. Overhead two Canadian geese honked loudly, flying low. He recalled that they mated for life and found a well of jealously rearing its ugly head. He had mated for life. What do they do when one partner is taken away?

The terrace red bricks were broken and sprouting weeds poked through. Walking slowly, he peeked through one of the many panes of wavy glass at the light blue ballroom. Counting three Schonbek chandeliers, he calculated their worth, whistling softly.

He passed the big room and realized it was the family's library. Still packed with books, it would be a nice touch for the open house. A roaring fire would really help when he did the showing. Pictures hung on green, blasé walls; overall, there was a feeling of faded wealth. Here and there were empty spots on the wall where he supposed Craig and his brothers took a family memento or portrait.

He sat abruptly on the first step, tears welling in his eyes. The bleakness of his life stretched before him as anger surged through his veins like hot lava. "You left me alone," he choked to the empty yard. "I don't want to do this," he whispered, feeling so small, adrift, and unhappy. His thoughts wandered to his kids again, and an overwhelming feeling of helplessness surrounded him.

Sighing, he wiped his cheeks, ashamed of the tears and surprised he had this incredible supply of them, and ambled over to the last set of French doors. The bedroom. The master bedroom. It was the crime scene; he had read the report on his computer. He saw the dusty outline of the grand furniture and wondered how well they were able to clean it. He rubbed a small circle in the glass, pressed his eye, and blinked.

"Oh my God!" Bile rose to burn his throat when he saw the carnage inside. Guts and gore splattered the room. Streaks of blood and holes from the shotgun pellets peppered the white walls. Bits of brain and decaying flesh decomposed on the floor.

A chair was overturned, its brocade drenched with stains of violence. The carpet was black with dried blood. A lone slipper, a pink thing doused in blood, lay abandoned by its wearer on the floor. Reeling away, he wondered if Melissa knew it hadn't been cleaned yet.

He started to run and fell into the bushes vomiting what little he had in his stomach. How was he going to look at that room with Melissa tomorrow? Stumbling to his car, he knocked over a planter with a dead bush. His breathing sounded harsh in his ears; he fumbled for his phone and dialed Melissa, his fingers shaking. It rang four or five times before she answered.

"Melissa?" His voice sounded strange to his own ears. "Have you been to the house?"

"Paul? Are you OK? Why?"

"I thought you said they cleaned it up."

"They did, Paul. I inspected it yesterday. It's all good, I promise."

"Um...you sure?" He blinked hard.

"Yes. What's wrong?"

"Nothing. Nothing. I'll see you tomorrow."

He dropped the phone in his pocket and sat in the car, stunned. Putting the keys into the ignition, he thought to drive away but stopped. He got out and warily went into the yard again. Wanting another look, now that he calmed his beating heart, he saw the small circle he'd cleared on the window earlier. Tentatively, his heart started pounding again as he approached the doors. Stupefied, he peered in and saw a stripped bed, wooden floors, and pristine walls. He shook his head then left quickly, wondering what the hell had just happened to him.

***

"I don't want it." Veronica's rotisserie chicken lay torn to small bits on her plate. Jesse at least had eaten his chicken but nothing else. Stella noted that everything on the plate was beige or yellowish. The kids bickered, fighting over everything from who got the drumsticks to who was using their personal utensil in the mac and cheese.

"It's full of your spit!" Veronica lashed out at her twin.

"No, it's not!" Jesse yelled back. Silver eyes glared at silver eyes, and Paul watched incredulously as Jesse prepared to hock a hunk of saliva into the mac and cheese.

"Don't even think about it, Mister." Paul stood up halfway from his seat.

"Veronica said I spit, I'll show her what—"

"No, you won't. Sit down." Paul spoke through his teeth. He was tired. How did Allison do this? His mind was still reeling from the bloody room he saw at Stillwell, so he missed the growing tension between his children. He had picked up prepared food on the way home, shuddering every so often, as the remains of the murder kept popping into his thoughts.

"I said," Veronica spoke more calmly, "use the serving spoon. Your fork is full of saliva—"

"It's enough!" Paul shouted. "You know behavior at the table. This is not going to be mob rule."

"What's 'mob rule'?" Stella was never one to let something interesting pass her by.

"Mob rule is anarchy, total anarchy," Veronica explained politely.

"Anarchy!" Jesse was white with rage. "I just wanted some macaroni. I am done." Throwing his fork down, he ran to his bedroom.

Stella looked at Paul wide-eyed, waiting to see the nuclear explosion at her misbehaving older brother. Veronica sighed and got up, ready to comfort her twin. "I really didn't mean anything. It's just disgusting. He was drinking milk straight out of the container this afternoon."

Paul stopped her with his hand. "Let him cool off. I'll talk to him later. It's not your fault," he assured her.

The girls chatted and he let the conversation wash over him. Though he heard every word, none of it registered. He would deal with Jesse after he had some time to cool off. He had missed all the cues when they got home from school. Locked in what he thought he saw this afternoon, their squabbles were mere noise. Stella poked him out of his reverie, and he looked down at his own plate. Mac and cheese, rotisserie chicken, and corn bread was not what Allison had in mind for a balanced meal. He didn't recall when he last saw Roni eat anything more than a slice of bread and butter. Stella had peeled a banana and told him that from now on, she was only going to eat foods in this color palate. Things were going to shit fast and somehow he didn't know where to start to make it better. And on top of everything, he was hallucinating bloody crime scenes and channeling creepy radio voices.

The phone rang, breaking the silence, and all three of them jumped. Paul started clearing the table, the phone propped against his ear.

"Hi, Mom. Just finished. No, she didn't eat much. OK, I'll try that. I'm fine. I said I'm fine," he repeated a bit too forcefully. "What did the doctor say? Of course it's no big deal, no, I don't want you to wait…" He watched Veronica sneak out of the room, leaving the mess to him. Only Stella stayed behind, her big brown eyes looking to him for direction. He smiled and motioned to the den, giving her permission to leave as well. "I know it will be fine. Yeah. OK, gotta go. Yeah, love you too." He hung up with a sigh then cleaned the rest of the kitchen in silence. This time he chugged Maalox right out of its container, just like his ill-mannered son.

He resolved to come to some sort of understanding with his children. Divide and conquer. Jesse's room was locked, so he jiggled the doorknob. He heard a muffled "night."

"Open up, son."

"I'm sleeping."

"Open up." Then he said gently, "Please." He rested his head against the door.

It opened slowly and his son's tear-stained face met his. Sitting on the bed together, they enjoyed each other's silence. It was different between boys. They didn't have to state the obvious. The TV was on. His breath smelled sweet from toothpaste, and a smudge left a trail on his top lip. Paul bent over and stroked his head.

"You done with that stuff in school?"

"I dunno. It happens. I get so mad."

"You were unreasonable at the table."

Jesse shrugged his thin shoulders. "Sometimes I think it feels better when I yell."

"I know. But it won't change anything and it just gets you in trouble."

"Mom wouldn't like for me to be in trouble," Jesse admitted, his eyes downcast.

"No, son, she wouldn't be happy about this."

Jesse grunted and settled under his covers. Paul sat on the edge of the bed.

"Do you want to talk to someone? You know, like a counselor?"

Jesse thought and then shook his head. "I don't want to talk to anybody right now. I don't feel like talking. It's like the words are stuck, here." He gestured to his throat. "You know what I mean, Dad?"

He stroked his son's head, noting it was matted with sweat. "Yup, I know exactly what you mean." He paused and crouched by the bed. "If you feel you want to talk, though, you know you can come to me." His blond hair touched the collar of his pajama shirt and curled under. He needed a haircut. Add one more thing to his list. Sighing, he thought for a minute and said simply, "You can get mad, but you can't take it out on others. Everybody's been very understanding."

Jesse looked down at his fingers that were pleating the blanket. "I just wish I could see Mom. I want to know if she's OK."

"Of course she's OK."

"How do you know?" Jesse whispered.

Paul looked at the ceiling wondering how to answer this, his heart breaking. Nothing in the books on parenthood he read prepared for these types of questions. Was she all right? He tried wrapping his head around the idea of Allison. Where was she? Could she be as brokenhearted as the rest of them? Was she resting in peace? How could she, really, when her life was here? Instead he assured his son, "She's at peace. Father Thomas said so. You believe Father Thomas, don't you?"

Jesse shrugged and replied, his voice small, looking so incredibly young, "What choice do I have? What proof do I have? I'm tired. I want to sleep."

"She's OK, I promise you, Jesse. I feel it here." Paul pointed to his chest.

"Then how could she leave us?"

He kissed his son, backed out of the room, and shut off itsthe light.

Veronica was still in the bathroom, so he tucked in Stella.

"You're up late, Stella Luna. Do you want a story?"

"Tell me about Mommy."

"What do you want to know?"

"Tell me about when you met her."

"I can't tell you that. I don't remember." He had known Allison his whole life.

"Try. Please," Stella pleaded.

He cleared his throat. "I never knew a time without your Mommy. If you are my stars and moon, she was my sun. You know, she lived next door to me growing up. We played together every day. Grandma and Nonni had coffee in the afternoon, and they would put us on the floor together and we would have adventures."

"Were you her hero?"

"All the time. She was the princess and I saved her from the dragon."

"Or an evil demon."

"Evil demon? What are you talking about?"

"You could save her from the evil demon who tries to take her away forever. You always save Mommy." Stella turned her trusting face up to him.

"When we were little, not now, Stella. There are no such things as demons."

"I don't think so." She looked up at him, her eyes earnest.

"That's enough of stories for tonight. Time for bed."

"Good night, Daddy. Now you are my hero." She settled into her bed.

Last stop was Roni who was drying her hair in her bedroom.

If Stella was the moon and stars, Roni was a rainbow. Sweet with a peaceful disposition, she never gave him an ounce of trouble. Until now. His serene child was troubled and couldn't find words to communicate.

"Ron, we have to talk." He was exhausted already.

"I'll eat more tomorrow. I promise." Intuitively, she read his thoughts. Although she and Jesse were the same age, Veronica seemed years older. She was a steadying influence on her more impulsive twin. "Jesse is bothering me." She looked at him with a grave face. "He is angry and it hurts me here," she said as she pointed to her stomach. "I can't feel anything else."

"I know it's hard."

"He is tearing me up inside, Dad. Can I tell you a secret?"

He nodded and closed the door.

"I'm glad Mom is gone. It was too hard to watch her. She wasn't the same person; she didn't even know us in the end. Is it wrong to feel relieved?" Fat tears welled up in her eyes.

"No, honey. No. I...I'm relieved too. The sickness was eating her up. She needed to leave."

"Why can't Jesse see that? Why is he so selfish? It hurt her too much to stay!" Veronica was sobbing.

He gathered her in his arms and put his chin on her blonde head.

"I know, honey. I know. It's hard to say good-bye."

***

At last alone in his bed, Paul hugged Allison's pillow close. Breathing in her light scent that lingered on the fabric, he didn't want her to go either. His eyelids were heavy, but his thoughts were too active to rest. The bed felt vast, an oasis of loneliness, the house silent, still as death. The air was still, heavy. A loud boom rocked the air, reverberating throughout the house and shaking the walls.

He shot up out of bed. "Jesse," he whispered, rushing out into the hallway. He peered through the gloom. "Is that you?" He moved to the kids' rooms and they were each fast asleep. Nothing had disturbed their slumber.

He walked through the long dark corridor. There was a strange mist that dampened his shirt so that it clung to his body. It was cold and his skin pebbled. He heard noise, a strange growling, that got louder as he walked through the narrow passageway downstairs, his back hugging the wall. He peered into the living room. The light had a strange glow that pulsed with a life of its own. He heard laughter, recognizing it at once to be Allison. He started to run toward the sound, but each time he felt he was close by, the sound came from a different room. He caught a glimpse of something in the living room, a shadow, hairy and foul, its wickedness a palpable thing. Allison hovered before him, her hair restored, blonde locks floating behind her, her cheek dimpled. Alabaster arms reached out to him; her lips moved, but he could not hear her voice. He ran recklessly toward her, his feet slipping, moving but getting nowhere. He was stuck. He gripped the carpet and tried to propel himself but couldn't gain any ground. He rolled toward a chair and crashed into it, taking it down along with a beautiful Waterford lamp. As the crystal shattered, it broke into tiny shards of glittering glass. He got onto all fours, and mustering all his strength, he leaped far, flying toward her. He realized out of the corner of his eye, something was catapulting toward him, a greasy ball of matted fur, huge and cat-like. It collided with him. Powerful arms grabbed him, but his sweat-drenched body slid painfully out of its viselike embrace. The impact sent him crashing onto the living room floor. Allison floated away; her face turned toward him in a mute appeal, the musty odor of something evil creating a wall of interference.

He came awake with a start, his heart beating wildly, sweat soaking his body. He got out of bed and ran to the hallway. The night was silent and all the kids were asleep. He rushed downstairs to see the living room. There was no sign of any struggle. The lamp was lit and whole; no glass carpeted the floor. No Allison. No freakishly big apish thing trying to rip him to shreds. He shook his head and went back upstairs. Acid bathed the back of his throat.

Reaching for the water by his bedside, he groaned at the pain, clasping his hand to his rib cage. His fingers came away red with blood. Three long tracks scored his skin. It looked as if a bear's claw had grazed the smooth skin of his side.

Shaken, he stumbled to the bathroom and examined his side. On closer look, it wasn't bad or really even that painful. It was just there. Paul stared at his white face, trembling with fear, for his wife, his children, and himself.

CHAPTER THREE
Tuesday

P aul woke up with a start. He never expected to fall asleep after that nightmare, but exhaustion had claimed him, and he slept for the remainder of the night. Glancing at his weary face in the bathroom mirror, he shaved and wondered if he should speak to somebody about it. He pulled his wife's ring from under his tee shirt then stared at the inscription, missing her, wondering what she would tell him to do. Should he get the kids into counseling? Did he need a shrink? Was he going crazy? Hearing things on the radio, seeing bloody crimes scenes, fistfights with Sasquatch in his living room. If he shared these things with a doctor, the authorities would take the kids away. He shuddered thinking of the ramifications of them being separated. No one was going to take his kids away from him, not ever. "Get a grip, Paul," he told himself in the mirror.

"Who you talking to?" Stella stood on her toes, her face level with his sink, her brown eyes searching. Holding her doll in her arms, she looked up pleadingly. "Are you talking to Mommy?"

"Stell…" He picked her up, resting her against his hip. "You know Mommy's gone. I'm giving myself a pep talk."

"What's a pep talk?"

"Well, it's like I'm missing my teammate, so I'm giving myself a little talk to snap out of feeling sorry for myself and get the day moving."

"Dad." Stella touched his unshaven cheek with her grubby hands. "Mommy is here. I know it. Just ask her what to do and she'll tell you. You have to listen."

He stared into her serious brown eyes, so much like his own, and kissed her button nose, told her not to be such a silly, and to get dressed. After she left he rested both his hands on the sink and looked at his reflection, muttering, "If it was only that easy."

Breakfast was an easier affair this morning. Paul seemed to get all their demands correct. Through heavy eyes, they all had a moment of giggles when the syrup opened and flooded the freezer-ready French toast. He introduced Roni to the wonder of peanut butter-covered French toast and was satisfied by the amount she ate. Even Jesse cracked a smile at his twin's delight. He had prepared oatmeal for himself; his spoon stuck straight up in the thick gruel. It was the heart healthy stuff Allison insisted he eat. Only hers was rich and creamy like velvet. A touch of sweetness—he had no idea what she used— kept him full the whole day. Choking it down, he wondered briefly what he missed on the directions. But there was one thing he certainly wasn't going to mention this morning…He wasn't going to say two words about the three scratch marks on his rib cage. Hell, he was so on edge every second of the day, that was all he needed to exacerbate the never-ending headache and freak out the children. *Kids, Daddy saw Mommy's ghost last night; Stella, you were right. She's there, but before I could say anything to her, a hairy monster attacked me. He sort of resembled King Kong.* Wouldn't go over well. All they had to do was share that with Mrs. Overzealous Principal. They'd have me locked up and on meds, the kids in foster homes, and pretty soon they'll all be peeing in their beds. He sat there, eating oatmeal, not tasting anything, thinking about what happened. This stuff happened in the movies. Whatever happened in your dreams, couldn't happen in real life. Could it? He was thinking about it too much and shook his head. He didn't notice, but the kids were staring directly at him.

"Dad?" asked Stella. "You OK?"

"You look strange," added Jesse.

"I'm fine. Everything is fine. Just thinking about how I'm going to sell this new listing."

"What is it?" said Stella.

He didn't want the kids knowing about Stillwell or its sordid reputation. He didn't think they would even know what he was talking about. "An old friend asked me to sell his parents' home."

"Who?" the ever-inquisitive Stella demanded.

"You wouldn't remember them." Paul dismissed the subject.

"I would," Roni offered. "Who, Dad?"

He never questioned his parents when he was young. Why did they make him feel like he had to report to them. The words left his mouth before he could stop them, "The Andrewses. Craig Andrews."

"Stillwell Manor?" Jesse asked with awe.

Paul's throat swelled shut. "How did you know about Stillwell?" he managed to sputter.

"Everybody in school knows about Stillwell. I go to school with Robbie Andrews."

"We both do," Veronica added. "That's Mr. and Mrs. Andrews's son. You know what happened to his grandparents, don't you?"

"OK, that's enough."

"The Andrewses were brutally murdered in…" Jesse started.

"Stop, Jesse."

"The old man's brains were splattered all over the bed—"

"Stop!" Paul slammed his fist on the table. His hand came a little too close to the oatmeal bowl and it flipped over like a pancake.

"What's 'murdered'?" asked Stella.

"Nothing," continued Paul. "I don't want to talk about it. Do *not* bring up the name 'Stillwell' in this house again. Do you all understand?"

"What happened at Stillwell, Daddy?" pressed Stella, with the lamentable lack of manners of the very young.

"Stella, enough. Do not say the name 'Stillwell' here. Does everyone understand? I'm not sure if I am even taking the listing, so we can all forget that name was ever brought up." The truth was, he needed this listing. All of his credit cards were close to being maxed out. Their savings had evaporated, and he knew deep down, he really didn't have a choice.

Mirabelle walked in breaking the uncomfortable silence. The kids got up, pulling on their backpacks without saying a word. Mirabelle placed her belongings in a corner of the kitchen, getting to work on the messy tabletop with her capable hands. Paul wondered who actually did the Stillwell cleanup. Sometimes all the scrubbing in the world would not make a stain disappear.

***

Driving to work, Paul's chest was sore, and he touched the scratches absentmindedly. They fit the outline of his hand, and he reasoned he must have gored himself in his sleep last night. There was no other reasonable explanation. He stopped at Starbucks and grunted a reply to the barista, and for a minute, wished he could wear a black armband, so people would leave him alone. In the past he knew the custom of wearing a token of a ribbon or an armband let society know the person was in mourning, aching, and brokenhearted and not in the mood for small talk. He couldn't understand how people didn't see he was changed. Each line in his face, the weariness of his shoulders, the sadness that surrounded him. Didn't the distant look give a clue to his mental health; couldn't they understand he didn't care who won the game last night? He wasn't interested in discussing the latest *CSI* episode.

He pulled into his office, parked in his new spot, and went to his desk. He had a pile of notes in Molly's handwriting. She had gotten him an appointment this morning with a young couple looking for a starter house.

"You're gonna take it, right, Paul?"

Molly glanced over her bright pink bifocals. "Jannette told me to give it to Evan. Screw her," she whispered.

"I don't want to take something from Evan."

"Screw him too. He don't need money. He lives with Mommy and Daddy. Take it, Paul. They're easy. Show them the Simmons place. It's been on multiple forever. They are desperate for a sale. This is a walk in the park for you. You can nail it."

He called them and made appointments for later in the morning. He left a message with Melissa Andrews telling her he planned on a photo shoot with a noted photographer in two days. He asked her to have gardeners clean up the weeds. His day was very condensed as he still hadn't gotten anyone to collect Stella from the bus. He could leave the twins alone for a short time, but at seven, he didn't want Stella to be a latchkey kid just yet. He knew Allison would have agreed. Staring at his computer screen, he pressed "escape" to get out of the program. The computer stalled. He banged the keys with frustration and tried to go to the next site and the computer went black then gray and turned on again. Pictures flashed crazily. Paul looked around to see if anyone noticed, but everyone's head was down, working silently. He heard the drone of conversation, which was normal; nobody appeared to have her or his computer taking on a life of its own. He looked back, and the images were going backward to colonial times. He saw soldiers, ballrooms filled with women and men with powdered white hair. There was music that only he seemed to be aware of, and he watched in horrified fascination as the pictures turned murky, cloudily distorted as if looking through a backward keyhole. The montage slowed and finally stopped, leaving a picture of the Stillwell wishing well on his screen. Surrounded by fronds of weeping willows, a light shone from its depths, illuminating the dark sky.

A cup of hot coffee was placed on his desk, making him jump with fright. Molly was behind him. "Sorry." She placed a reassuring hand on his shoulder, her red nails resembling dripping blood. "I didn't mean to startle you." She bent over and looked at the image on his screen. "Ugh, the Stillwell wishing well. I hate that place."

His nerves felt raw as if doused with acid. "I have to meet Melissa Andrews there at ten this morning. Why? Why do you hate that place?" He tasted the coffee, letting it calm him, and the last dregs of his fatigue melted away. She made a face at that. "What? What do you know about it?"

She rolled her chair closer to him and sat down, her voice a low whisper. "It's silly."

"So what? Come on. I think it might be a white elephant," he complained then stated it might be a whopper to try and get rid of.

"Well," she said then looked around, making sure no one could hear them. "They say it's haunted."

A chill ran up Paul's back and he shook his head.

"Come on, Molly, that's a load of crap. They say that about all the old estates. Sometimes, that even draws the gothic crowd in."

"No, listen, I dated one of the Andrews brothers back in the eighties." When he looked at her skeptically, she retorted, "The uncles of your friend, not his brothers. I could have been a child bride, you know, if it had worked out."

"What? Which one, Anthony or Charles?"

"What do you think?" She winked. "The handsome one, of course. Did you think I would sell out for money?" She giggled.

There were three brothers, Craig's dad, Richard, Anthony the middle brother, a big contractor on Long Island, and Charles, the youngest, a hotshot lawyer from Manhattan. They had all since married and moved to different areas of the state, except for Craig's parents. "They all had money. They bathed in it."

She said, "Well, there are different degrees of money. Charles always told of a family ghost. Someone from the Revolutionary War time. She was rather famous, Hannah Andrews. She was beautiful, the daughter of the first Andrews who built the house. She did the unthinkable. She fell in love with the enemy. A debonair captain in Washington's army."

"*The* George Washington? Dollar bill George Washington? So what, they were American. She should have loved an American."

"Ah, but there's the rub. The Andrewses were Loyalists."

"You lost me, Molly."

"Loyalists. Supporters of the British. The Andrews family served King George. His daughter was entertaining famous British nationals and meeting her lover in the back by the Stillwell wishing well." She added as an afterthought, "They housed British soldiers there during the Revolutionary War."

"That sounds creepy. I don't know how I'm going to rehabilitate this house." His old friend, acid reflux starting making his presence known. Paul rubbed the spot below his rib cage. Molly handed him an antacid after rooting around in her purse.

"You should see a doctor about that." Molly nodded to his stomach.

"It's nothing. Tell me more."

"It gets even worse. He forbid their courtship, so Hannah disappeared. They couldn't find her for months and hung her American lover as her murderer. They claimed he was a spy for the colonists. They found her remains years later at the bottom of the well. Her ghost and her lover's ghost have haunted the place for over two hundred years."

"I don't think I want this listing."

"Oh Paul, you don't believe in ghosts, do you? Hey, it's almost ten. Don't you have to meet Melissa Andrews?"

He pulled out of the office, his mind on the horrible story of that house. It would be a massive commission, the house should sell in the multimillions, and the hit would bring him back, but the whole thing made him uncomfortable. "Ally, Ally," he called to his wife, wishing he could hear her advice. "What should I do?"

***

The landscaping company was already working on the long drive when he pulled in. A crew of ten or twelve guys were taming the wild bushes and trimming trees. The place looked much more inviting. That was fast, he thought, feeling better about the listing. Melissa and Craig waited for him by the front door. He noticed that Craig had ripped off the last of the police tape and had wound it around his hand. They looked miserable. If body language was an indicator, he would guess theirs was not a marriage made in heaven.

He got out of his BMW and met them on the top step outside of the massive stone entry. "Who first?" Craig held out his hand. "Sorry about Allison. She was a nice girl." He was tall, with white blonde hair and dark eyes. Dressed in a golf shirt, he guessed this meeting pulled them out of their country club. Craig was preppy handsome and Paul never quite understood why they became friends. He was everything Craig Andrews was not. Brought up in a Waspy household, Andrews had nothing in common with the very Italian Paul. Where Paul's house was all warmth and friendliness, the Andrews home was proper and cold. Melissa was wearing a tennis outfit, her skirt just skimming her tight butt. She stood close to Craig, but her eyes drank Paul in.

"I really liked your parents. Terrible shame." Paul avoided her gaze, feeling a bit like a sheep in a lioness's den.

"Unbelievable. Selfish and just reprehensible to leave us with this scandal. I don't understand my father."

"Do you know what happened?" Paul asked.

"No, it's unexplainable. I thought they were happy. He was so proud. Always took the high road, even when he fought over money with his brothers. Nobody can believe this."

"Yes." Melissa shook her head. "He was such a quiet man. Never liked attention of any sort. It's so strange."

"He snapped, Melissa." Craig turned to his wife.

She responded, "We thought they were so in love. The police haven't ruled out an intruder."

Craig raised his eyebrows. "There was no intruder."

"How about we go inside and discuss a strategy?" Melissa held out a huge round ring with an antique skeleton key on it. Paul took it and felt the heavy weight of it in the palm of his hand commenting, "Is this original?"

Craig shrugged and said, "My father always held on to tradition and never wanted to change anything in the house."

Paul gestured to the painted black door with a huge brass knocker imported from England close to three hundred years ago. He stared at it noticing a gargoyle etched into its surface. It was worn but distinguishable.

"Are you married to this knocker?" He pointed to it.

"It's as old as the house," Melissa said. "Why? Oh, eww, what is that? A dragon?"

"A demon," Craig answered. "The family demon. You don't know about it? Geoffrey Andrews had it made for the house when he built it. According to the legend, it guards against evil."

Both Melissa and Paul answered in unison, "No," and Paul finished with, "It's gotta go."

They entered the spacious entry with its black-and-white marbled floors in a beautiful two-story hall. Period furniture was placed along the white walls. It was elegant, grand, and cold.

"I would bring in a big bouquet of flowers for the entry on this table; it will warm the place up." He pointed to a regency-burled, walnut round table. "We could say the blooms are from gardens on the estate. People will love that. Makes them feel like landed gentry."

"Nice," Melissa agreed.

Craig smirked as he shrugged his big shoulders. "Whatever."

Paul went to hand the key to Melissa who shook her head, "You keep it now. You're going to need to get in here to show the house. Is that alright with you, Craig?"

"I don't care," Craig said. "Make sure you don't lose it. They're hard to copy."

"Do you have another?"

"There are a few floating around. The housekeeper has one, I have the other," Melissa assured him as he pocketed the cumbersome key.

"Had they updated the kitchen?" Paul asked as they walked down a narrow hallway lined with Sheraton consoles that could have paid for both Veronica and Jesse's college educations. They must be sitting on two million dollars in antique furniture alone, he thought to himself.

Paul stopped just outside the billiards room, his eyes drawn to a broken white marble tile. Craig looked back, smiling when he noticed what caught Paul's attention.

"Oh man, did I get my ass kicked for that," Craig said.

"What?" Melissa came to stand next to them. "Oh what happened here. I've never noticed that."

Both Paul and Craig grinned in shared amusement.

"They never let me into the main house after that," Paul murmured.

"Superbowl, 1995. We appropriated some of my Dad's brandy..."

"And scotch, and vodka, I'd kill my kids if they did that..." Paul added.

"Well, Carey, Dad's butler caught us and we dropped a case of really old..."

"Scotch. What a mess. We cracked the tile and I was banished to the pool house when I visited," Paul finished.

"All my friends were."

"I wasn't," Melissa said pointedly.

"You were special," Craig said sarcastically.

The kitchen had been redone in the late 20s and was still the same putrid shade of green with white utilitarian cabinets. This was clearly going to have to be gutted and will take away from the value of the house. Everyone wanted gourmet kitchens today. The appliances however were new and had the capability to do banquet catering. Paul jotted notes into his spiral notebook.

They gathered at a picture window, admiring the overgrown garden. As Melissa and Craig were momentarily distracted by an antique jug, something flashed outside, its laser beam hitting Paul directly in his eyes. He gasped and Craig looked up saying, "What? What is it?"

"Did you see that?" Paul asked.

"Did I see what?"

"The light."

"I didn't see anything," Craig replied and the subject was closed. They walked through the rooms, and when they approached the master, Paul hung back just a bit. He did not want to go in there. "I swear, they cleaned it, Paul. You wouldn't even know something happened in there."

"Why?" Craig turned to look at him. "What's the matter now?"

"Nothing. Nothing at all." He followed them in, his heart tattooing his chest.

Sure enough, the room was spotless, and the chair he had seen from the window, missing. A scent of something familiar assailed his nose and he gagged. It was the unmistakable smell of illness.

"Your mom was sick?" he asked Craig.

"No. Why?"

"Just asking." He knew what he smelled and the odor was of illness.

Craig and Melissa stood in the center of the room, hands clasped. She put her arms around him, but her face looked at Paul. Craig returned her embrace and didn't see her predatory eyes following Paul as he backed uncomfortably out of the room. "I'm going to run upstairs and check out the other bedrooms." He recognized grief in Craig's expression but refused to acknowledge what he saw in Melissa's glance.

He ran up the grand stair case steps two at a time and walked around each bedroom. Using his cell, he took a few shots so he could come up with ideas later. Each bedroom had been redecorated in a different time period. It was actually pretty interesting, Paul thought. There was a suite from the roaring 20s which was all fringe and lace in muted colors. The art deco room had mirrored furniture and he laughed thinking Stella would have a field day in there with the multifaceted vanity table. There was a regency style bedroom that looked right out of the set of *Pride and Prejudice*. He went back to the rooms over the servant's wing, here the hallway was dingy and unused. The carpet was so worn that it bordered threadbare. It was eerily quiet, not even the floor boards creaked and he felt removed from the rest of the house, in a time warp. Ghostly shadows of furniture under Holland covers unnerved him each time he opened another door. The last bedroom on the right was closed off, the door stuck, its handle difficult to move. He pushed it with all his weight against the door, and it gave in, propelling him into the room. It was painted in old colors, sort of a sea foam, as if it hadn't been updated in two hundred years. There was an ancient tester bed, hung with yellowed lace. He touched a corner then watched it disintegrate into dust. The room was musty, old, and silent. He walked to the window and looked out on the yard seeing the Stillwell wishing well right in the center of his view. Tucked in a small dale, it was flanked by lush weeping willows. A broken bucket swayed on worn rope lines. It was an eyesore, he thought. Maybe he should suggest Craig call his uncle and have the place torn down for condos. An eerie chill swept up his spine, and sweat dotted his forehead. The ring on the chain around his neck vibrated with a life of its own. It grew hot, the heat singeing him. "This can't be happening," he muttered.

He made a hasty retreat for the stairs, overwhelmed by claustrophobia. He reached the carpeted landing and raced down the steps. Midway, he felt a punch to his back right shoulder blade, knocking the wind from him. The stairs came up to meet his face as he tumbled down the rest of the way to rest dazed at the bottom.

He became aware of a cool hand first and muffled voices next. Craig's white face was talking into a cell phone.

"Yes, that's right, the Stillwell estate, off Route 25A. Right away. He's breathing, oh, Paul." He knelt down. "You OK?"

A hand restrained him. "Don't move. The ambulance will be here soon," Melissa added.

"No." Paul raised himself painfully. "I'm OK. Just dazed."

"What happened?" Craig asked.

"I..."

"It's that blasted carpeting. Craig, I told you we should pull it up!"

"I think I was pushed." Paul heard the words come out of his mouth.

"The EMTs will be here in a minute. Did you hit your head?" Craig handed him a bottle of water he had gotten out of his car.

"I don't think so. I don't know. Maybe." He looked up at them. "I don't know if I want to do this listing. Maybe I'm not ready."

"We'll wait. We don't want anyone else," she added hastily.

"Paul." Craig looked at him. "I…I know you're going through a rough time. Nobody else wants the listing. Nobody else will take it. Buddy, I need a favor."

He shook his head to clear it, rising. As he stood he brushed imaginary dust from his pants, trying to find words.

He hated being put on the spot. He wanted to say, *I'm seeing things. My head's not screwed on straight right now. Don't ask this of me.* But the money beckoned. A commission to put him back where he wouldn't have to worry about expenses. He couldn't stop the next sentence that came out of his mouth. "Cancel the ambulance. I tripped. It was nothing."

"Are you sure you're OK?"

"Honestly, a bit embarrassed, nothing more." They shook, walking out into the morning sunshine.

The back of his head hurt like the devil, throbbing with a life of its own. He swallowed two aspirin he kept in the glove compartment. Then he headed back toward town, insisting he was fine and could drive alone.

What's happening, he thought. No matter how badly he didn't want this listing, the more he kicked and screamed, the more the house was sucking him in. Paul knew it was a punch to the shoulder. He felt it. He could feel the clenched fingers as they impacted his body.

Paul wanted to be done with Stillwell. The trick was to move it quickly, so he set up a broker open house for Friday, to be followed by a public open house the next day. Calling a caterer all while driving, he then phoned Molly to arrange for the professional photographer to do a spread for the *Times* and other high-end magazines. He avoided turning on the radio.

He realized that lunch had come and gone, and while he wasn't hungry, the overriding grief had eased a bit. The heaviness in his chest was still there but concentrating on other things relegated it to the background. His indigestion had also subsided.

***

He pulled into the library, parked, and found himself limping slightly to the double doors. It was a tiny building, off the main street of town with a musty old smell. The librarian looked up when he entered. Surprisingly, it was packed with older people sitting on old mustard-colored vinyl seats, reading books and newspapers.

"Where can I find records on the old houses in the area?" he asked.

"How old?" She had a rusty voice to match her wrinkled face.

"I want to research Stillwell Manor."

She paused, her lips pursed. "Are you a reporter?"

"No, not at all. I'm a realtor. The house is for sale. I thought a bit of history..."

"Just so." Her face cleared. "I knew the Andrewses. They were lovely people."

"Yes. I grew up with Craig, their oldest son."

"You know, it's not what people think," she whispered while leaning in close. The unpleasant odor of mothballs and mint surrounded her.

"Excuse me, what?" he asked, confused.

"Richard loved Maryanne. He would never have done such a horrible thing to her." She shook her head and tsked. "They were so in love." She placed a hand on his arm, her fingers like talons. "He would never have killed her." Her faded blue eyes searched his.

"I...I wanted to do some research on the family that lived there during the Revolutionary War."

"Oh," she said and smiled, "you don't need a book. I can help you. I am the local historian as well as the president of our DAR."

"What ?"

"DAR, Daughters of the American Revolution. My family is distantly related to the Andrewses; we've been neighbors since the seventeen hundreds. My family is Newfield. You know, as in Newfield Mall."

"Newfield Mall?"

"My family owned that tract of land. It was farmland and my parents sold it to developers in the fifties. I live in the original gatekeeper's cottage. Oh, these old homes, they do have tales to tell." She was excited now.

"So, what do you know about Stillwell Manor?"

"It was named for the wishing well in the rear. Have you seen it? Squire Andrews was a Loyalist; in other words, he supported the king, as did my ancestors. This whole area supported King George. The squire had a daughter, whose name was Hannah. She was beautiful. I have a portrait of her in one of the books somewhere. I'll find it for you. But I digress. She fell in love with a local boy by the name of John. John Wendover, of the Hicksville Wendovers. They were a rebel family."

"Rebel family...you mean 'patriot'? He was a patriot. This was during the American Revolution, not the Civil War," Paul interrupted.

"Yes, I know." She smiled. "Depends on which side of the pond you sympathized with, dear boy. Anyone who went against the king was a rebel. They were revolting against their own country. You only become a patriot if the rebellion succeeds, otherwise you're a traitor. John joined up with Washington. He was carrying information about troop movements. So they say...Well..." Her eyes got dreamy. "...her father wouldn't have it. No, no, not at all, no rebel was going to marry his little princess."

"What happened to them?" he asked even though he had most of the story from Molly. It sounded like the historical bodice rippers his mother read all the time.

"It was a tragedy. Terrible. Hannah disappeared, and they blamed the boy." She leaned closer as if sharing gossip. "He was charged with treason, but they say he was framed by Hannah's father who blamed him for his daughter's disappearance. He was hanged at the corner of High and Bauer streets."

"Here! In town!"

"Well, we are talking close to two hundred forty years ago. They didn't lock children up in their rooms. She was very young, seventeen or eighteen. He couldn't have been more than nineteen. Years later, they found her remains in the well on the estate. They say when he couldn't have her, he threw her down the well," she added with relish. "Wait here. I'll bring you a picture of her portrait. The artist was pretty famous, studied under Lawrence."

The old woman floated away, while Paul digested the information. His phone rang and he answered, much to the disgust of the locals. An older man pointed to the "no cell phone" sign, while a woman shook her finger at him.

It was Molly. Before he could tell her he couldn't talk now, she started, "You're late. I went to all that trouble of getting that young couple for you." Her voice whined through the receiver.

"Crap. I'll be back in twenty. I had to make a stop. Can you keep them busy by filling out forms?"

"You owe me, Paulie, big time...I had a nail appointment...Paul..."

The older woman returned, an enormous book open in both her arms. He caught a glimpse of the subject of the painting. Absentmindedly, he dropped the phone onto the counter.

"I know, I kn..."

His gaze froze on the page of the open book.

"She was a beauty." She propped the book on her desk and moved away, her thin finger pointing to a woman that took his breath away. Paul pressed Allison's wedding band close to his heart as if to stifle the ache there. Dressed in a billowy, white dress, hair loose and flowing, glinting blonde in the sun was his wife, Allison.

"Paul...Paul..." Molly continued on his discarded cell.

He swallowed thickly. Staring at her beloved face, he read the caption: "Hannah Andrews circa 1775 Stillwell Manor by R.G. Fontaine. Late daughter of Squire Geoffrey Andrews, presumably murdered by her lover, John Wendover."

"Can I take this?" he asked.

"No, it's reference." She looked at his tense face. "Why?"

"I am trying to sell the house. An uncle in the family wants to tear it down. I want to create a cleaner history for it."

She closed the book firmly. "Here. Anything that preserves the old homes of Long Island is important to me. Don't tell anyone I gave it to you." She put her hand over his. "But please return it in the same shape."

Paul did something unexpected. Leaning over, he kissed her powdery cheek. "I will guard it with my life."

***

Racing back to his office, he glanced at the dash and realized he was a half hour late. The couple sat beside an animated Molly who entertained them with local lore. "And here he is the man of the hour."

"I apologize. I got stuck at another house." Molly raised her thin eyebrow at him. "Did you prepare those comps for me, Mol?"

"Does McDonald's have golden arches?" She handed him a sheaf of papers. "Simmons house first. It's got everything they need. That's the ticket."

"Do you want to follow or go in my car?" he asked as he walked them out.

Though the shock of the portrait was on his mind, somehow he was able to get them to commit in record time. It was the Simmons house, just as Molly suggested. The buyers came up, the sellers came down, and a sale was in the works a scant two hours later.

"Man, you're good," Molly admired. "What the heck happened to you today?"

"Nothing."

"What are you, Jesse now? I can see something is on your mind."

"Wait here." He ran out to the car to retrieve the book. He motioned for her to go into the privacy of his cubicle. "Take a look at this."

He opened the page and spread the book on his desk and heard Molly's gasp.

"Allison?"

"Nope. That's Hannah Andrews. Weird, right?"

"I'll say. Melissa Andrews called here earlier to see if you're OK. What happened over there?"

"I don't know," he said absently as he stared down at the picture. "I was coming down the main staircase, and...I don't know, it was nothing."

"What? What?"

"I think I was pushed."

She slapped his shoulder, and he winced. "Get out of here. Did you hurt yourself?"

He shrugged. "Only my pride. I may just have tripped on the carpet. It's old."

"You're still taking the house?"

"I feel like I have to. I don't have a choice. I need the money." He closed the book and headed home, ready to tackle dinner for his three kids.

"Get normal. Get normal." He repeated this mantra to himself in the car. He was afraid to turn on his radio. This was crazy. Seeing crime scenes, being pushed by ghosts, a demon who chose to visit him nightly—was this the new normal Allison spoke of? He breathed deeply, slowing his racing heart. I have to be normal for the kids, he thought wildly. Just my imagination, he convinced himself and then said out loud, "I am having a nervous breakdown."

***

He came home to a packed house. His parents and in-laws sat in the brightly lit kitchen, the table groaning with trays of home-cooked food. His mother got up when he entered and grabbed his face.

"You OK, Paulie?" She kissed both his cheeks, looking at the shadows under his eyes. Her thumbs caressed his tender skin. Feeling his throat clog, he stifled the urge to throw himself on her deep chest and cry. He felt his face heat.

"Ma!" He pulled away. "Albert, June, Pop." He nodded to each of them. Albert was short with a thick head of silver hair and Allison and the twins shared his eyes. June was as spare as his mother was fat. They were old friends, acting like sisters. His father, a little more stooped than before, was tall for his age. His hair was thinning but still there, and Paul hoped he would have the stamina his father still possessed when he reached his age.

"I made gravy." His mother started ladling pasta and sauce into a plate.

"Ma, stop. I'm not that hungry."

"You don't eat enough," she complained.

"I brought you pot roast." June started making him another plate. "It's your favorite." She had gotten old while her daughter was sick. He noticed her hand was shaking.

"I'll eat when the kids get here. What's going on?"

"Junie and Al are leaving tomorrow. They wanted to see you and the kids." His mother was pulling out yet another casserole from the oven.

"I'll stay if you need us," his mother-in-law added, eyeing him. He liked them, really liked them; they were sweet. It was just too much to have them around. He didn't have the strength to take care of them. His reserves were tapped and running on empty.

"Thanks, Junie," he called her by her childhood nickname and she smiled sweetly. "I have to get things going here."

"I know, sweetie." Her voice cracked. Al rubbed her back. The room got silent.

"It's hard. It's so hard." She cried and that did it for everybody. After they all wiped their tears, the silence became more comfortable than conversation.

The screen door opened and Stella ran in, a wealth of people who adored her in the room. She didn't know where to start.

"Grandmothers first then the grandpas," Paul told her and smiled as she launched herself into his mother's arms. She gave each grandparent her or his due, brightening the atmosphere. She threw her backpack in the corner. Paul made a mental note to check it later.

The twins followed shortly after, and the table became greasy with comfort foods. He was happy to see all his children eating their meal heartily, which differed greatly in color. They even scarfed down the vegetables. He had to remember to find out what his mom did to make them taste good. Jesse grabbed more eggplant with his fork, caught Paul's eye, and picked up the serving fork. Paul smiled, winking to his son, who winked right back, his silver eyes sparkling. He was a rare devil, his son.

"Nonni," Stella asked his mother in between mouthfuls of meatballs, "wasn't Daddy always Mommy's hero?"

"Oh, your Daddy was quite a knight in shining armor, right, June?" His mother beamed.

"Of course. I remember once we had a freak snowfall and he carried Allison home from the bus on his back. They went out in spring clothes; you know they didn't report weather as thoroughly back then. I think Ally was wearing knee socks—oh her legs were so red with the cold. They were frozen stiff, but he wouldn't let her walk in the snow drifts," June recalled, smiling at him.

Paul ducked his head.

"They would have swallowed her. She was such a petite little thing. How about that time when that kid, what was his name, the Lloyd boy, you remember. He kept stealing Ally's lunch." This was from Paul's father.

"He decked him," his mom said with pride.

"He *what?*" Jesse asked, his mouth filled with food.

"Ma!" Paul shouted then turned to Jesse, "Don't talk with your mouth full."

"Yeah, but Ally had her moments too. Remember the pool?" June asked his mother.

"Oh my God, how could I forget it." His mother sighed.

"What? What pool?" Paul asked, starting to clear the table, wondering where he was going to store all this food.

"You drowned," his father said and the table became silent. "We almost lost you."

"When? I don't remember."

"You were six or seven, so Allison was just over five. We had a little kiddie pool in the yard. You were splashing and slipped. I didn't see it. I was cutting some basil in the garden," his mother added. "I should have been watching you."

"You were right there, Arlene. It was just a second," his father assured her.

"Allison saved you. You banged your head, landing in the water. You were out cold. She grabbed you and pulled your head out all while shouting for me. She was so smart," Nonni added, "such a good girl."

"I don't remember." Paul cleared his throat, his voice almost inaudible.

"You saw a white light, you told us."

It seems my father is a wealth of information today, Paul thought.

"One, two, three...Here it comes," Paul counted to himself.

"A white light!" Jesse shouted, his face beaming. "You saw *the* white light?"

"I don't remember anything," he answered. As far as he was concerned, this subject was off limits.

"He saw the white light." His mother shook her head knowingly. "And Allison saved him, so she could marry him someday. Who wants cake?" His mother got busy with desserts.

The sugar rush left the kids giddy, happier than they had been for almost six months. They pretended to be circus performers and jumped from couch to couch in the den. Their laughter brought tears to his eyes, his loneliness a tangible thing. Had Allison been there, they would have traded glances, eyes meeting in shared enjoyment in love with the kids' antics. His sister called during her break to check up on him, so he spoke to her while he loaded the dishwasher.

"Man, it's like the work never ends. Fill the dishwasher, clean it out, laundry, food shopping, we're out of bananas. I need a clone."

"That's called a wife." The instant she said it she regretted it. "Hey, I'm sorry."

"Stop, Lee," he assured her. "We are not gonna spend the rest of our lives pretending something didn't change. I'm still me and..." He thought for a way to explain what he wanted to say. "I don't want you walking on eggshells around me. I'm tougher than you think."

"It's not that, Paul. It's so raw."

"It will always be raw."

"I promise you it won't. The first of everything is tough then you set up new routines and finally there comes a day when you can't remember exactly when Ally was there or not there."

"And you're speaking from your vast experience."

"Divorce is a type of death too," she said and paused, her voice thick. "At least you've got the kids. Billy took our dog."

"I always said he was a bastard."

"Love is blind. Don't lecture me tonight. I have to go back to work. I...It was really hard at first. Our friends melted away. I know what it's like to be alone, and the one thing is, Paul, you are not alone."

He felt tears burn the back of his eyes. He couldn't speak, but he wouldn't let his sister know. Swallowing hard, he said softly, "I wish I didn't have to be here."

"But you do," she said. "Those kids need you. Allison doesn't."

He thought for a minute and said, "Lee…"

"Yeah, what Paul?"

"Did…Do you ever…" He didn't know even where to start. How do you share a nervous breakdown? "I don't know. Nothing…"

"Paul. Allison was your life. This is going to be hard. You were so close." She paused and he heard her swallow. "Listen, a lot of the time it made me jealous."

"Jealous? You're crazy." No I am crazy, he thought.

"You don't understand. She was your world and nobody else mattered. You never needed anyone but Allison." Lisa paused. "I'm not bitter about it. I'm glad one of us had that kind of love."

"Maybe I'd be better off if I didn't love her so much."

They were both silent and then Paul began, "Lee, I'm having dreams. Bad dreams." He paused weighing whether he should share all the information. "Sometimes even when I'm awake." There he said it. Did he feel relieved? Not yet.

"Paul. It's normal. Grief comes in so many ways. You are exhausted. Maybe, maybe you need some medication."

"Nope. It's just dreams. No medicine. I don't want to get on that train."

"Depression can do lots of strange things. How about a bereavement group? You know, at the Y."

He sighed, and she heard his despondency. "I don't have time. I don't have time for this."

"Look, I've got to go back. If you need to talk, call me later. I'll be home by two."

The kids surrendered easily to bedtime, and Paul got the book out of the car. Their bellies full, they appeared content. He visited their rooms, kissed each good night, and was satisfied most with Jesse, who seemed to be more at peace.

"I still miss her, Dad."

"You're always going to miss her, Jess. Know that she's around you all the time."

"I wish I could believe that," Jesse said wistfully as he shut off the lights.

Paul thought, so do I, but chose not to share.

Making sure he was alone in the den, he opened the book to the page of the portrait of Hannah Andrews. Her luminous face stared up at him. He then pulled an old photo album from the bookcase and found a picture of Allison at eighteen. There were subtle differences; a dimple that Ally had was missing from Hannah's cheek. A dainty mole decorated Allison's upper lip. The hair was off by a shade and Hannah was softer, where Allison had the toned body of an athlete. His head cupped in his hand, something nagged at his memory. It was ten o'clock and his in-laws might be sleeping, but they were leaving too early for him to wait for tomorrow. He dialed their number, and his mother-in-law answered, her voice low.

"Paul, is everything all right?"

"Everything's fine, June. I'm sorry I'm calling so late, but I have a question that can't wait. Did I wake you?"

"No, dear. I've been having trouble sleeping."

He grunted in agreement.

"Yes, I know you understand. What is it?"

"I know your family is from the area. Do you know how long?"

"Well, Al's family came from Poland. They farmed on the east end for about four generations. There is still a cousin who sells strawberries to the Hampton crowd."

"Really?" He appeared politely interested but wished she'd get to the point.

"Why do you need to know?"

"Stella has an ancestry project." Where did that come from, he wondered. "She forgot to ask about it at dinner. I couldn't answer some of the questions. So Al's family has been here how many years?"

"They arrived in the early teens. Oh, about 1914 or so. Now the Bakers, that's my side, we go back hundreds of years. In fact, you know Baker Street in Cold Spring Harbor?"

"Sure."

"That's named for my five-time great grandfather. He was a...What did they call that a...barrel maker."

"Cooper."

"Exactly. For the ships out here. Now my mother's side, they were Irish and in service. You know what that means."

He didn't have a clue. "Not at all."

"Her family came over from Europe with an old family here. You were friends with one of the boys. I never liked that family. The Andrewses. She worked on the estate as a maid. I'm ashamed to admit this."

He fell back onto the couch silently. He had a funny feeling where this was going.

"Paul, please don't share this with the children. My family has always been embarrassed by it."

"What, that someone was a maid?"

"No, my ancestor had an affair with Geoffrey Andrews and I am the descendant of that ill-fated union."

He stared at the two pictures, speechless. "Whoa," he choked out.

"You're not upset, are you?"

"Don't be silly, Junie. It doesn't matter to me."

"Well, in truth, it may not have been an affair..." Her voice became a low whisper. "It's been passed down that she was not a willing participant, if you know what I mean. I'm glad you asked. I never told Allison, but now, I don't know, I don't want the story to die with me."

"Do you want me to share it with the kids?"

"When the time is right, I suppose." They sat in comfortable silence. "You know Ally loved you from the day she was born. She was always meant for you. And you were meant for her. I never saw two people as in love as you and Allison. She used to watch you; her great, silver eyes followed you everywhere. There was that time, you remember, when you started college."

"Huh," he agreed. "I never meant a word of that. I thought that was what I was supposed to do."

"It broke her heart, when you told her you wanted to date others. 'Mom, he belongs to me,' she would tell me. I told her that if she really loved you, she had to let you go."

He tried to say something, but his voice failed. "I didn't mean to hurt her."

"You were a kid. And you needed to sow those wild oats."

"She let me go. She understood. She cried so hard."

"But you returned, as I knew you would."

"So I did," he whispered.

"And look at the beautiful family you made together. Paul, you will see her again. I promise. But you have work to do here."

"Work, work, work, work, work," he said playfully. "June, you have no idea how much I miss her."

"Oh yes I do, my boy, oh yes I do." Her voice brightened, and she said, "So you'll come down with the kids for Easter?"

"Either presidents' week or Easter, depends on how the holidays fall. You'll be back for Christmas?"

"We wouldn't miss it."

"Safe drive, June."

***

He sat in the darkened room, the TV illuminating his face. "Wow" was all he could say. So, there was nothing spooky about the resemblance between his wife and Hannah Andrews. No hocus-pocus; they were related. Distantly but definitely. They shared a gene pool that created a likeness, nothing more. Maybe, he could file the freakish coincidences away into the X files. Dreams, depression, like his sister said, grief explained it...

A scream of pure horror split the peace of the house. Without thinking, he ran to Jesse's room to find his son knuckling his eyes, screaming his throat raw. Sobbing, he reached blindly for his father, curling up against him.

"Shhh, Jesse, what's the matter? Stop..." Paul cuddled his son.

"It was this thing. This horrible—" He hiccupped and could barely continue. "It smelled so...Oh Dad. It had Mom. She was trapped and it was growling. I could see her; it had big, hairy shoulders and a tail..."

"Stop, a dream. Nothing more. Do you want a drink?"

"I'll get it." Veronica stood in her nightgown at the open door. She turned and Jesse calmed.

"It was horrible. Mom is in trouble," he insisted.

"No she's not, Jess. She's OK." He held his son at arm's length. "Have I ever lied to you?" He studied his child's tear-drenched eyes.

Jesse shook his head, still trying to stifle a sob.

"Thank you, Roni." He took the water from his daughter. "She is fine. She's watching over us making sure we follow all her rules. Mom couldn't be anywhere else. This is where her heart is."

Jesse looked at him skeptically. He tucked in his son, wrapping him in his quilt, staying beside him until soft snores told him the night terrors had vanished. Quietly, he eased out of the room leaving the door open a bit wider. Veronica came next.

"He's all right. Just a bad dream," Paul said as he walked her to her room. "The dreams feel real, because we all miss her. It will start to get better."

"Why, because we will stop missing her?" she demanded, her eyes wounded.

"No, sweetie. We will always miss Mommy. It's just as time passes, it gets less. It hurts less."

"I don't know if I want it to hurt less,'" Veronica whispered.

"What?" He asked her, "Why?"

"Because if it hurts less, maybe we're forgetting her."

"Oh baby, you're never going to forget Mommy. You're..." He kissed her head, tears stinging his eyes. Maybe he did need help with this. It was beyond his capabilities as a parent to answer his children. Jesse was seeing the same hairy monsters he was, Stella was talking to the dead, and Veronica held her grief to her like a blanket, afraid to let it go. "I just know we'll never forget Mommy, but the pain will ease."

She rolled over, closed her eyes, and was instantly asleep.

Now I need a drink, he thought. He walked over to the group of bottles they kept in the living room in an improvised bar. He headed straight for the Scotch, pouring two fingers and draining it in one gulp. How am I going to do this? How could she leave me? How could I bring up three kids alone, without a wife? His angry thoughts boiled in his head. Furious, he smashed the glass into the sink, regretting it instantly. Stella walked sleepily into the kitchen. "What happened?" she asked.

"I dropped a glass. Go to sleep. It was nothing," he told her.

He felt the liquor start to warm him, welcoming the numbness it would bring. He poured another glass, went to his bedroom, gulped it down, and threw himself on the bed. The lights were out, the room pitch dark, the house silent. He heard his own breathing; his eyes drifted shut and then he knew nothing.

He was in an endless corridor. Mist swirled around him, wrapping him in tentacles of coldness, making it hard to breathe. He heard his raspy breath near his ear, the fetid smell assailing him. Pushing forward, he started to run, and Allison stood at the far end of the tunnel. She was floating, dressed in white, her face twisted in pain or horror. Arms flailing, she urged him closer. He saw her mouthing the word, "Hurry." Running as fast as he could, again he felt trapped, as though he wasn't moving. Stumbling, he pushed up, and from the corner of his eye, he saw a great hairy thing barring his way. He could not see if it was man or beast, but he reared back in horror when a great serpent tail lashed out at him. He felt the sting of its whip-like flick strike his cheek. He forged forward, but a powerful fist bashed him sideways and he hit the wall, where he fell and rolled backward. Undaunted, he got up, his voice dying in his throat when he saw Allison dragged off by the creature. "Noooo!" he screamed, climbing up smooth walls, grasping at the hairy back, coming away empty handed. He jumped and landed on its back; the thing clawed him with fury. Hands pulled him around and shook him like a rag doll. The beast grabbed the chain around his neck, gripping it until it strangled him. His eyes bulged as his airway constricted. The chain ripped his flesh. Lights danced behind his eyelids, and then suddenly, there was blessed relief. Cool water rained down on his face. He opened his eyes to his terrified daughter splashing him with water.

"Dad, Dad..." Veronica whispered. "Are you OK now?"

He stopped her hand and looked around the room. His palms wiped the water from his eyes as he shook his head. "Bad dream. Even grown-ups get them. Go to sleep." He caressed her soft cheek. "It was a bad dream, Roni. I'm fine. Go to sleep."

Reluctantly, she left the room. Paul stumbled to the bathroom, turned on the light, and prepared to wash his face. He dropped the washcloth and stared at red lines bruising his neck. "What the fuck..." He touched the tender skin. "What the fuck is going on?"

CHAPTER FOUR

Wednesday

The next day, he dressed with care covering up the bruises with his high-necked button-down shirt. Some of Allison's makeup covered the parts that peeked above his collar. He fed the kids and got everyone off to school. Jesse was solemn, almost standing in the shadow of his twin. Veronica watched both Jesse and her father, her silver eyes big in her white face. He had to do something; the grief was making them all crazy. They'd end up locking them all up. Stella hung back, her brown eyes wide and staring at him.

"Daddy..." She came up close.

He bent down and came face to face with her. "Do you think I can go to dance again? I had to stop when Mommy got sick, because no one could take me. I really want to dance again."

He touched her soft cheek. "Of course, Stella Luna. I'll set it up. If I can't take you, I'll get Nonni to do it." He realized that Allison's illness had robbed them all of a normal life. When she first got sick, they mobilized to get all the treatments going. Both sets of parents helped, as well as his sister; her nursing skills proved to be a lifesaver for him. But the kids became casualties of the cancer too. Keeping them in school was all he could do; every ounce of time, strength, and money, every resource went to Allison. Reiki, special food to tempt the invalid, massages, therapies, you name it—they all pitched in and no one, as well as no expense was spared. None of it mattered in the end. All the special diets, medicine, and then the more advanced medicine made each day a living hell as she was tortured into living. Sores covered her body, her hair fell out, light hurt her eyes, but they kept trying more and more things, knowing she was terminal, but doing everything to prolong her life until finally the empty husk that was his wife, faded and slipped away.

He pressed both his palms against his eyes and tried to blot out the final images of her parchment-like yellowed skin and her eyes sunken into their sockets until she resembled the living corpse she had become. Why did they do it, he wondered. It had reached a point where she didn't even know they were in her room, but there was always one more thing they could try, and they did. Until finally, she held up her hand and whispered, "Enough, let me go," and he did. Tears pricked his eyes and he swallowed the lump in his throat. "I can't," he told her. "Please..." she whispered back, her lips dry and cracked.

He would set up dancing for the girls and basketball for his son, today, for sure. It was time for the kids to live again.

***

"Dreams. Dreams." He convinced himself but still refused to turn on the radio. They were influencing each other. How else could both he and his son have the same dream? Veronica was holding onto it, to keep close to her mother, and little Stella always had an active imagination. His mother-in-law's startling revelation explained so much, he reasoned. It couldn't be anything else. They had to get out more. Today he would turn over a new leaf. Today he would try to get his head out of his ass.

He stopped for Starbucks and took the time to buy a piece of lemon pound cake and remembered to savor the tart sweetness on his newly awakened taste buds. He found himself actually enjoying something. It was the first time in a long time he desired something and he noticed it didn't taste like ashes.

He got to work, pulled in, and Molly joined him at his desk. She looked over his shoulder to his notes. She became aware of an exposed scratch on his neck. "What this?" She touched his neck with a pointy red fingernail.

He ducked his head. "I cut myself shaving."

"That don't look like a shaving cut to me." She rolled her eyes. "The photos of Stillwell Manor came in. I emailed them to you today. Let's have a look."

He opened the file and sat back to look at the artistry of the photographer. He told him he wanted to make sure they got in the fall foliage of the surrounding trees. It would look like a painting out of the Hudson Valley school. They both leaned forward as the pictures came onto the screen.

"What the hell is that?" Paul pointed his finger at the screen. "He must have had a dirty lens. This is inexcusable."

"Oh shit!" Molly exclaimed. "I don't like this. I don't like this one bit."

"You better believe it. That fancy photographer you picked cost a small fortune and we have to pick up the whole bill. It was in the contract with the Andrewses."

"That's not dirt," Molly whispered. "Look at the wishing well. That's not dirt." Her shocked eyes looked at him. He peered closer to the picture. A white haze surrounded the well. "Spooky" was the word that came to mind. It was thicker at the bottom and wispy toward the top. It had the image of a person, but a skeptic would have thought it was a smudge on the lens. From the group of pictures that were taken of the facade, one had a caption put there by the photographer, next to the bedroom window: "I thought you said the house was empty." It was written underscored with lines.

"Oh my God, Paul, look at that window." Molly pointed to the last bedroom, the one overlooking the well.

He held his breath. No, no, no. It couldn't be, he thought, but he turned to Molly and said, "Don't say it, just don't say it."

"But it's Allison," Molly whispered into the shocked silence.

"It's a double exposure. It can't be real. These things are *not* real."

"Look at the picture, Paul. You can't imagine that away."

"Wait a minute." He started loading pictures he had taken with his phone. He had about twenty. They started combing through them and when they got to the last bedroom, standing beside the bed was a faint outline of a woman with Allison's blonde hair dressed in a colonial-era gown.

"This is unbelievable. Do you see this?" Molly demanded. "You have to get the house cleaned."

"Melissa had it cleaned. She hired two crews."

"I don't mean that kind of clean. We need a psychic cleaner."

"Oh come on, that's a crock. We don't need to pay some crackpot to burn incense," he shot back, disgusted.

"It has to be a reflection or something."

"A reflection of what? Your imagination. How did it get there? You see it plain as me," Molly whispered fiercely.

"This can't be real, Molly. You know this can't be real. There has to be a reasonable explanation. I'll be back later." He threw on his jacket and went to his car. He was going to see for himself what was going on in Stillwell Manor.

"Wait, Paul. I have a friend I can call." She yelled out to him as he left the building.

***

The house had some activity, a few box trucks were parked outside, and he realized furniture was being taken out of the house. Melissa stood next to her car, a dark blue Bentley, smoking a cigarette. He noted uneasily that she had a way of sucking on a cigarette that made him sure he knew the one thing Craig loved about her. In fact, he had a hazy memory from his youth that she gave the best blow job in high school. He shook his head and shifted where he sat, uncomfortable with the mental image. Where did that come from, he wondered. She was taller than Allison, with a wealth of luxurious mahogany hair. She threw a notebook into the car as he pulled up, her smile wide.

"Hi." She had a deep voice, her eyes sparkling, and Paul recognized that she was flirting with him.

"Hi Melissa, where is Craig?"

She frowned while tossing her head. "Left for LA. He's got a girlfriend, you know."

"Sorry to hear that."

She shrugged. "He can't divorce me. It'll cost too much." She laughed. "Did you know that I am the one with the money?" She walked over to his car and leaned in, her breath grazing his cheek. She smelled of wine, and it made him faintly nauseous.

"Actually, no," he responded, pulling back. He wanted to add that he really didn't care. "What's going on?"

"Some of the pieces are very old. I want them in my own house." She moved away as he exited the car. "I want to make sure I get them before Anthony grabs them. They are expensive as well as original." She picked a piece of tobacco off the tip of her tongue with two elegantly French manicured nails. Her eyes lazily searched his face.

Paul rested his gaze somewhere far from her, refusing to make eye contact. She leaned against his car, jutting her hip out to him suggestively.

He knew her house; he had sold it to them four years ago. They bought it before the crash and had overpaid by at least a million. It was a huge postmodern colonial, the ones that sprung up all over the North Shore of Long Island in the late nineties. They were all getting dated, too old to move, since the current trend was for sleek, utilitarian modern homes with Zen-like grace. Opulence was out, and they were going to be stuck with their home for some time. Unless they chose to take a bath on it.

"What are you doing here?" she asked him, her green eyes glittering.

"The photographer took shots and I'm not happy with them. I wanted to inspect the rooms again."

"Was Hannah in them?"

"Excuse me?" he asked, stunned.

"She shows up at the most awkward times, ruining everything. You should see our wedding pictures. I should have known then, it was going to be no good." She reached out to fondle his tie.

"What are you talking about?" He smoothed his tie from her hands; she had his attention now. She moved closer and spoke in a sultry whisper. Her lush lips grazed his ear. She was in his personal space and made him uncomfortable.

"The whole family is cursed." Her voice was husky. "When Hannah died, it's like the house became possessed. Nothing good ever came out of it, including Craig."

"You don't believe that, Melissa. Do you?" This time he looked her full in the face, challenging her. She backed off a bit, subdued, perhaps a bit angry.

She stared at him without expression then ground out her cigarette on the gravel driveway. "Sure, of course not." She paused. "I know a place if you want to go," she added, looking at him slyly.

"Nah. I don't cheat, Melissa."

"I do," she shot back. "You can't be cheating. You're not married anymore."

"Just a formality. I'm not interested."

"Pity."

"Not to me," he responded. He was not new to this. Many times bored housewives had come on to him. He really wasn't interested, not now, not ever.

"Do you mind if I have a look?"

Her eyes opened wide with pleasure followed by surprise. "Oh, you mean there." She gestured to the open doorway. "The house. Be my guest. I don't care." She walked toward her car. "You have my number, Paul. If you change your mind."

He shook his head.

He turned and bounded into the open hall. "Watch the steps." She laughed and took off in her car, spewing rocks and gravel in her wake.

Paul entered the house as the last worker left; the door closed with a resounding slam.

He turned, noticing the chandeliers dimmed then brightened. He wore shoes today, and the heels clicked hollowly on the floor, seeming to echo in the empty house. Wind whistled down the chimney, and for once, he said to himself his next house would be brand new, without a history.

He walked into the library then stood in the center, drinking in the comforting smells of books, cigar smoke, and peace. This room drew him, like a moth to a flame, but instead of warmth, he felt safe. Though it was quiet, it was nonthreatening, peaceful. He rested in an oversized chair, closing his eyes, letting his fatigue wash over him. No ghosts, no hairy apes. He walked to the overstocked shelves and pulled out a book. Allison would have loved this, and he wondered if the greedy Melissa knew she had an original signed copy of *Thomas Paine's "Common Sense"* in the library. He considered what other gems were hidden here. If he were a less honest man, he'd have pocketed the book. It had to be worth a small fortune. An atlas lay opened on a huge desk. It was at least two hundred years old. Troop movements were outlined. Squinting, he realized it was the plans for the Battle of Brooklyn, the very first battle of the Revolutionary War and a defeat for Washington. He recalled from his store of school trivia information that it was one of the biggest conflicts of the war. This stuff should be in a museum, he thought, feeling privileged just to be looking at it. His eyes scanned the tall shelves, noticing one book not aligned with the rest. It was as if someone had pulled it out but not returned it all the way to be flush with the others. Its spine came just over the edge of the bookcase calling to him to come and get it.

He reached up and couldn't grasp it; it was so high. He ran to the billiards room two doors down. They hadn't taken the pool sticks, so he took one and brought it back to the library. Reaching up with the stick, he pushed the book and gingerly moved it, until it flew off the shelf to land like a wounded bird on the floor. It was an account book, written with spidery handwriting from centuries past. Leafing through it, he saw modern stationery, white against the parchment-colored pages of the book in the rear. He glanced around and opened it, his breath whooshing out of him.

It was a note from Craig's father. Paul scanned the letter. He addressed it to his children apologizing for what he was about to do. It wasn't right, he knew, but life had left him no choice. He loved their mother, he wrote, but she had Alzheimer's, and they had been able to hide it for only so long. Craig's father was not feeling so well either, but his wife was in the home stretch. It was undignified, ugly, and the medicines were not working. If something happened to him, she would have no one to take care of her. She was afraid to be alone, and so it seemed was he. She had asked him, insisted that he help her. She didn't want to live anymore. Well, it seemed Craig Andrews's father didn't want to live without her either. All his life he worried about scandal and had punished anyone in the family when he or she brought unwanted attention. He was very sorry, but there was no easy way out for them. He would try to be as neat as he could. To shoot his wife, it took some guts. Taking his own life would be easy. He was sorry, he loved them all, but life just wasn't worth it without their mother to share it with him.

Paul fell into the chair, his heart heavy for the older man. He knew exactly how he felt. Man, he was lucky; he went with her. He pulled out his chain and rolled the band between his fingers. It was warm and comforting, like holding onto his wife's hand.

He took out his phone to call Craig but found his voice wouldn't work. He folded the letter and placed it in his shirt pocket and sat in stunned silence.

Was that love, he pondered. Killing his wife so that she wouldn't suffer then choosing to join her rather than stay alone. How often in the darkest hours of Allison's illness, did he find himself thinking the same thing. Only the kids kept him here. His kids.

He got up and approached the staircase. Carefully he climbed the steps, keeping close to the wall. The house had a presence; he knew it, felt it deep in his bones, but he refused to admit it to himself. He went straight for Hannah's room. It was cold, so cold. He swore he saw his breath in the air. The door opened more easily, its hinges screaming in the silence. If this wasn't spooky, he didn't know what was. He walked to the center of the room and turned around.

"I know you're here," he heard himself say. It felt surreal; he didn't believe in ghosts.

"Did he?" he asked himself.

There was nothing, just the aching cold of loneliness. He missed Allison with his heart and soul. He walked over to the window and leaned his head against the glass, watching the wishing well in the garden. Sighing, he looked up at his reflection. A gentle breeze drifted down his neck, making goose bumps ripple his flesh. The curtains were moving gently, swaying as if disturbed. He refocused and saw behind him, a ghostly reflection. He stood frozen. It was Hannah.

He spun and turned only to find an empty room. Chills ran up his spine. "Where are you? Come out," he shouted to the bare room. "I'm losing my mind."

***

He raced out of the house, slamming the door so that it locked behind him. Driving faster than he usually did, his mind replaying the ghostly specter. He couldn't get a grip. Was it Allison, or was it Hannah? Was it real? He couldn't tell the difference anymore.

He punched in Molly's number on his cell and her voice filled the car. "Where are you? I have to get ready for an agent's open house. You're supposed to be there with me. I don't like the house; she has a big dog."

"I just left Stillwell. Where's the listing?"

"Ryan Court. Follow the signs," she added. "You know the blue-and-white ones."

"I said I'd be there, Mol. Don't nag," he snapped.

"Whoa. Welcome back. I was wondering where that guy was." He was known for his temper. He was easygoing and charming until his buttons were pushed and then he had the potential to boil over. It didn't happen often, but when it did, he could become volcanic.

"Sorry. I didn't mean to yell. I'm not having the easiest day."

"Talk to me, Paulie."

"I'll take you up on that. I'll be there in seven minutes."

"Hurry. I'm freezing my ass off. You gotta put that dog in the basement."

***

It was a farm ranch, run down, near bankruptcy. If he wasn't so scattered, Paul might have bought it and fixed it up for resale. He and Allison had talked about doing that, but her illness sucked up everything this past year. Now he didn't have time to take a crap, let alone invest and try to get a rental business going.

Molly paced the long driveway, her strawberry curls cascading down her back. She was older than him, her late forties she said, but she hung out with a young crowd. She loved Van Halen and made it to every local concert, dragging her friend Fiona, everywhere. She was hard drinking, hard loving but kindhearted, and he adored her.

"Frickin' dog. He jumped on me when I opened the door. I'm a mess." She pointed to a rip in the fabric of her flowing skirt. "I love this skirt. That beast ruined it."

"I'll give you half of my commission," he joked, took the key, opened the door, and commanded the dog to sit. He did obediently, and he turned to Molly with a smirk. "I don't know what you're talking about. Look at this guy. Docile as a dove."

"More like a vulture." She shuddered. "I just don't like animals, unless they're two legged." She smiled widely.

"Forget it, Molly. I'm still taken." It was an old joke between them.

"Shucks!" She snapped her fingers, following him into the house. "You look like you've seen a ghost. What happened at Stillwell?"

"Hah!" he roared. She smiled. It was the first laugh she had heard out of him for almost a year. The humor chased the lines from his face, and he looked younger, more carefree. He was gorgeous. Allison and he had made a beautiful couple, like the ones in magazines. He was tall, with rich brown hair. Swarthy skin and soft chocolate eyes, he was a thirty-six-year-old hunk, Molly thought. "Such a waste." She sighed, lamenting to herself that though she adored him, he only had eyes for Allison. She was always in the wrong place at the wrong time. If he were only ten years older, or she ten years younger.

"Hungry?" She redirected her thoughts. "I have a tray of muffins in the car."

Paul ran out then carried in both the cellophane tray of gourmet muffins and the jug of expensive joe. "Let's put it on the island."

She was digging through her purse. "Got it!" she exclaimed, pulling out a small bottle of vanilla extract. "The house stinks of wet dog."

"It is pretty bad."

She started rooting around for a tray. "I know she keeps aluminum pans in here. Aha."

She pulled out a tray and filled it with tap water and poured half of the vanilla in the liquid.

"Open the oven," she ordered.

He opened the oven door and turned the dial. "Three fifty?"

"We'll be smelling like we're baking cookies in no time."

He corrected her. "Muffins."

"What?" she asked, puzzled.

"Baking muffins."

"You are such a purist, Paul. So…" She pulled out a sheaf of sign-in papers, busying herself with setting up her station. "Tell me about your morning."

"I met Melissa at the house. I think she came on to me," he said then paused. "I know she came on to me."

"Never good to mix business and pleasure."

"Agreed. I don't like her. There's something cold about her. She's so bitter."

"I rented out the cottage on their estate for them a few years back. You were handling a commercial job for the firm. She was a bitch then, so I wouldn't be surprised that she is a bitch now."

"Look what I found in the library." He unfolded the letter and they read it together.

She sniffed. "You know I never liked Richard. He was a nasty bastard. He wasn't happy when I dated Charles. He had problems with my age and oh yes," she said, her eyes light with amusement, "he hated that I was a Buddhist back then."

"You were a Buddhist?" He broke off a piece of muffin and offered it to her.

"Yes, for a while." She took the muffin and continued. "That was my Asian phase. All the Andrewses are snobs. Even your friend Craig. They think they're better than anyone else. Wouldn't let the kids play with anyone who he didn't feel was proper."

"Well, Craig hung out with me." He shrugged.

"Never understood that, you know. It must have been the mother's influence. It is kind of sweet that he loved her so much," she added wistfully.

"I wonder if I could have done that."

She stared back at him, her face a mask of horror. "You have young kids. It was out of the question."

"It's hard, Molly."

"Let's eat another muffin. Don't you love lemon poppy?" She stole another off the tray, and they shared it.

"Do you believe in an afterlife?"

"Yup. Always have. Do you?"

He shrugged. "Never thought about it. I hadn't been to a funeral since my grandparents died twenty years ago. I haven't thought about mortality. It was so far off."

"I hear you. I was on the fence for a long time. I was born Catholic then I lapsed. In college I flirted with Buddhism. It lasted a long time, freaked my parents out. Now I'm kind of universal. I am at peace with all religions. I take a bit from here and a bit...Oh hello..." She welcomed an agent to the house and her professional side took over. He let her show the house, and for a while, they had no time to talk. He glanced at his watch; it was coming on two and he'd have to leave.

They cleaned up once the last of the realtors had left. He let the dog out and then helped Molly put the heavy aluminum sign in the back of her car.

"You never answered my question. Do you believe in ghosts?" he persisted.

She looked him in the eye, her face serious. "I have a friend. Her name is Georgia Oaken. Oh, I see you've heard of her. Don't make faces, Paul." She put her hand over his. "See her first then take her to Stillwell."

"That's unethical."

"Tell Melissa and Craig you have to do a psychic cleansing." He reeled away, and she grabbed his arm. "No, stop. Listen to me. Maybe you need the psychic cleansing. If you don't believe, it's an evening of entertainment. If you connect—" She stopped to make sure he was listening, really listening. "—you hit pay dirt."

"She's a whacko."

"That's her stage personality. Do I look like I would hang out with a wacko? No, don't answer that." She kissed his cheek and told him. "That's it. I'm calling her for you. You can meet her at my place on Friday. Will your sister watch the kids?"

"My mom, my sister, someone will watch them."

"Good." She peeled out in her red Mustang convertible.

***

He made it home two minutes before Stella. He stared at the raw chicken he had defrosted in the fridge this morning. It was disgusting; he wished he could just feed them hamburgers every day. Slap them on the grill, put in a bun, and done. What could be easier. Picking up the poultry with his thumb and forefinger, he grimaced at the texture. Slimy, who wants to eat this, he wondered. The phone was cradled against his ear, as he set up dance lessons for the girls for Friday after school. Stella slid a filthy hand onto the counter to steal from the open bag of cookies.

"Go wash, first," he ordered with a stern glance. Her hands were a mess. What did Allison do with her nails? He hadn't touched them since she was a baby. By the time they had a third child, Allison pretty much did everything with ease and confidence. Both their mothers were nearby and helped all the time. But her illness had aged them all. Maybe, he'd ask his sister to take the girls for manicures this weekend. He had to get Jesse a haircut. It was too long. How was he going to fit everything in a twenty-four-hour day?

He roasted the chicken, cooked rice pilaf, Veronica's favorite, made frozen peas, though nobody would care for that, and tore up a rudimentary salad. He perused his feast with pride and wondered for a second if Allison knew how hard he was working.

Eating was subdued but not oppressive. Jesse had dark circles under his eyes. Clearly exhausted by his night terror, he was complacent, easy to handle. Homework was tackled, baths, and rather than let them disappear to their rooms, he invited them to sit like a pack of wolves, entwined on the couch, their body heat keeping each other's feet warm. *Man v. Food* was blaring from the television. Nothing was more comforting, and it distracted them, seeing a dude scarf down huge chunks of food to the chagrin of his fans. All four of them fit together, chocolate chip cookies and milk and a weird feeling of peace.

Jesse hesitated by his door and looked at his father's eyes. Paul winked. "Call me if you need me."

Jesse nodded and slept through the night.

Paul did not. He had the dream. It started differently this time. Her body fit perfectly next to him in their bed, the soft lines of her figure pliant in his hands. He felt Allison stroke him, her fingers surrounded him, making him hard and ready. Reaching out, she slipped away to be dragged down the corridor. He saw her hands flailing. The mist rolled in, obscuring the monster, Allison's screams echoing off the walls. Paul's rage roiled through him; he raced after them, only to have them elude his every turn. Exhausted, his breath rasping in his ears, he grabbed and clutched a handful of the monster's matted hair. Allison was slung over its back, her face white and frightened. She called to him, but the guttural growl smothered her voice. The fight was clumsy and slow. Paul felt more powerful, as though he almost had the fiend. But the greasy fur slipped through his fingers, leaving him to finish the night alone.

CHAPTER FIVE
Thursday

He woke heavy eyed, weary to the bone, dissatisfied, and feeling broken.

"Suck it up," he told his reflection in the mirror. He put on his game face and got the kids out in an organized fashion. He had to admit with pride in the fact that they were coming to the end of the first week and had ironed out so many difficulties. He wished the dreams would stop, though. But maybe they weren't dreams; perhaps they were something else. While he knew to all outward appearances he looked functioning, deep down he was beginning to worry that there was a message in the dreams. Was the beast holding Allison back? Did she need Paul's help? Like the time he had rescued her from the deep snow, did his wife need his help now? Was she trying to get a message to him about the monster holding her captive? Could any of this be real? Logically, he reasoned that his love for her created dreams, but why would she be in jeopardy? Unease filled his heart, his sense telling him she was in trouble. Could the dreams be telling him he had to do something? Paul shook his head. Like he told the kids, they were dreams, wishful thinking, his mind reaching out for the woman he loved. So, the other half of his brain asked, if it's wishful thinking, why would Allison be terrorized?

Maybe Molly's psychic will have an answer, he thought then laughed to himself. He didn't believe in that kind of crap.

Paul dialed Craig while he was sitting at the table having his coffee. "Can you meet me?" he asked.

"I'm in Manhattan. Is seven OK?"

He hesitated. "I'll make arrangements." They picked a bar and hung up.

He called Molly. "I'll be a few minutes late today."

"So what else is new?"

Dry cleaners, grocery, and lastly the dance store to pick up outfits for the girls and shoes to match.

While driving he arranged for Jesse to be in the Saturday league for basketball, and he was so busy, that by the time he pulled into work, he realized he hadn't thought of Allison for the latter part of the morning.

"I did it," Molly informed him.

"Did what?" he asked absently as he went through his mail.

"I got Georgia. She'll come to my house Friday night. After that you can decide if you want her to do the cleansing."

"OK." He looked up at her earnest face. "I really don't know about this."

"How much proof do you need? You saw the pictures. I don't know what's going on in your house at night, but I know you well enough to know that it's something strange."

He looked away. "Grief is a funny thing. It messes with your mind. OK, OK, I'll see your nut job."

He called his mother asking if she would watch the kids Friday night.

"Why, what are you doing?"

"I have to do a business thing," he said evasively.

"You know I will always be available to you. What time?"

"Molly, what time?"

"You're going out with Molly?" his mother asked.

"Ma. I said it was a business thing." He felt heat move up his neck to color his face red.

"Seven." She called out excitedly. "I told her to be here at seven."

"Seven. Oh crap, Ma, I have to meet someone tonight. Can you watch them tonight too? I won't be long."

"Don't cook. I'll bring supper."

"Great. I know the kids will be happy."

***

He left work early and took a drive to Oyster Bay. There was a little hole in the wall that they used to go to when they were teens to buy gyro. It was one of those places that had a special way of cooking it and he knew the owner well.

He hadn't been there for over seven months and when he walked in, Nick, the owner, put down the rag he was holding, came around the counter, and held out his hand.

"Mr. Paul..." He had a thick Greek accent, iron-gray hair, and a vintage mustache. He called to his wife who was singing in the rear. "Leni, Mr. Paul is here. We was just talking about you."

Paul shook his hand warmly.

"I'm coming," she called out. "Give him coffee. He loves your coffee."

"Thanks. I'll take a gyro. I'm starving," he said, surprised that he really was hungry.

"You want to take some for the wife, the kids?" Nick rushed to the counter, picked up a sickle-shaped knife, and carved paper-thin slices from the hunk of meat grilling next to the stove.

"I make moussaka for you!" Leni called out from the kitchen, and he recognized the clatter of pots.

"Where you been, Mr. Paul? I thought you moved over to Spiro. My gyro better, no?"

He slid into the counter. "Yeah, well. My wife got sick."

Nick halted. "She OK now?"

That was a good question, Paul thought, but replied, "No. She passed away last week."

"Oh my God. Leni, get out here." He put down the knife and came to take Paul's hand. "I don't believe it. She's such a good girl. So young." He tsked. "What happened?"

Leni stood in the door, her face white with shock. "Oh, Mr. Paul, I'm so sorry."

He sat with them for an hour, telling them about the illness, and they told him funny stories about the two of them, how they enjoyed watching their budding romance, seeing them married, and the family grow.

"It's a terrible thing." Nick refilled a glass of ouzo he had pressed on him earlier. "I lost my wife too."

"What? Leni is your wife."

"My second wife. My first wife die in a car accident in Greece. I left because I couldn't drive that road no more. I kept seeing her on the road. You know," he whispered, "dead."

"Yes!" Paul leaned forward. "Me too. I keep seeing Allison. What ended up happening?"

Nick looked around to make sure his wife couldn't hear him. "I never go back."

Nick and Leni pressed care packages of food on him, which he reluctantly took. It seemed to make them feel better to be doing something for him. They insisted when they saw his half-eaten sandwich grow cold on his plate. He promised to return with the kids the following week.

***

Nonni and Grandpa had dinner on the table by the time he got home from work. They told him to take his time getting home; they would be there for the kids. Lisa sat on the couch braiding Stella's hair. Veronica, quite the housekeeper, was helping her grandmother put out plates on the table. Guess they wouldn't be eating off paper tonight.

Jesse was in the garage showing his father his fishing rod. Plans were made for a trip to the pond on Sunday.

"What are you doing here?" Paul asked his sister.

"I switched shifts. You OK?"

He nodded and smiled at the pretty picture his daughter and sister made. "I got stuff in the car. You want to help me?"

She got up and followed him outside. "You look tired, Paul."

He shrugged. "I gotta ask you something. Don't... Don't judge me. Do you believe in ghosts?"

"Whew. Paulie. That was the last thing I expected from you."

"I know. I know." Brown eyes studied brown eyes. "Well...do you?"

"Noooo," she said finally. "I see terrible things every day. Things that God himself would have never approved. And if he did...I can't believe in something like that. I trust science, and you can't marry science and spirituality. Science is the truth. Spirituality...is for nuts."

"You make sense."

"You're just missing Allison."

"You're probably right."

***

Dinner was festive and it did Paul's heart good to see his kids happy. He left before the cleanup, to meet Craig. He was early, so he sat down and ordered a beer. Snacking on peanuts, he observed the women lined up at the bar, predators looking to mate. They eyed him, and he looked down, not wanting to make eye contact. He was not interested.

Craig arrived twenty minutes late. "The LIE was a parking lot. I hate the commute. How you been?"

"You know. Sucks."

"Yep. You were together a long time. How is it going with my sale? I presume this is why you called."

"Actually no. Two things." They were interrupted by the waitress who got Craig's order of whiskey straight.

Paul reached into his pocket. "I was at the house, and well, I was in the library. I noticed a book was hanging off the shelf. I shouldn't have looked in it, but I did and this was inside. I thought you'd want to read it."

Craig took the letter and read it, his face emotionless. "Well, well, well, this all fits. I got the autopsy reports today. My mom was far gone with advanced Alzheimer's. They never said a thing." He paused. "They were always a private pair."

Paul didn't like him; he was clinical about the whole thing. "Yeah. I'm still sorry. But trust me, as sordid as the shooting was, watching what they did to Allison was horrible."

"You would have still done the treatments?" Craig asked.

"When you get the diagnosis, you're willing to do anything. Then the options narrow until you are suffering so much, you just want it to end." Paul never looked up from the table.

"I'm sorry about Ally. She was an amazing woman. You said there was something else."

"Would you be offended if I did a psychic cleansing of the house?"

A deep rumble of laughter erupted from Craig's chest, causing the women to glance at them. Craig appraised a leggy blonde and smiled. She smiled back and Paul knew his friend would not be leaving alone tonight. Craig raised his glass, motioned to the bartender to fill hers, and gave his attention back to Paul.

"You believe all that ghost bullshit?"

"Some strange things have happened. But, really, the house has a reputation. I can say we've done a cleansing and it should help with the sale." He added as an afterthought, "Your wife seems to believe."

"Huh. The only one possessed is Melissa. She's a she wolf. Ever hear of a succubus? No, I can see that you haven't. A succubus is a demon that sucks the life out of men when they sleep. I stopped sleeping with Melissa many years ago."

This was too much information for Paul. Craig continued, "As long as you get rid of the eyesore, I don't care what you do."

He sat stunned, not knowing if he was talking about the house or his wife. "I thought you guys were happy."

"*Were* is the operative word, here, Paul. Marriage isn't made for our lifetimes. Back when people had shorter life spans, the love lasted. It's easy to love someone for ten years. Twenty…tough. Thirty…fucking impossible."

Paul gestured to the letter that Craig had left on the table. "It looks like it lasted for your parents."

"An aberration, I assure you." Craig dismissed his parents' long marriage and apparent love for each other, as well as their final sacrifice.

Pensively he wondered if he had the chance, would Allison's and his love have lasted? He was sure it would have. He felt attached to her, as if an invisible cord connected them, tied them to each other forever. She was a part of his very soul, like they had been joined at birth. Every time he saw her, it felt like he belonged, like he was coming home. She was as much a part of him as his arm, his heart. She was the other half of his soul. A great wave of loss washed over him, and the bleakness of life without Allison stretched before him. Craig's abrasive voice brought him back.

"I think we outgrew each other. Time for something new and improved." Craig smirked. "She is as unhappy as I am." He shrugged. "Matter of time. How much?"

"How much what?" Paul choked on the last of his beer. He thought he was asking him how much time was left for him to stay with his wife.

"How much is the psychic cleaner going to cost me?"

"I haven't asked yet. Can't be more than a few dollars."

"Send me the bill. Gotta go." He slid out and walked over to join the woman at the bar.

Paul pulled out of the bar, feeling jumpy and unhappy. It was not yet eight o'clock, but it was pitch black. Something nagged at the back of his mind, so he drove to Stillwell and parked in the driveway. Walking around the back, he used a flashlight to find his way to the well.

He felt drawn to the place, as if a presence was calling him there. The air was still, not a sound to break the velvet darkness of the night. He pointed the flashlight into the well and peered down. It was deep, dry, and cloaked in shadows. The walls were made of cobblestone, with flecks of mica reflecting moonlight back at him. The light bathed the darkness and he stopped. There was something in the wall, but it was close to the bottom. He couldn't make out what it was, but it shined back at him. Frustrated, he glanced up to the bedroom window and saw the curtain shift, but not before a pale face stared down at him. He couldn't make out the features, but it was there. He rubbed his eyes, blinked really hard, and looked again. The face was still there. It pulled the curtain shut and moved back, never taking its eyes off him.

Allison's ring felt heavy around his neck, weighing him down.

He went to the house in the back facing the well and opened the door.

"Hello?" he shouted. Just then, he heard footsteps running in the hallway upstairs. "Hello?!"

He swung around to the front hall and looked upstairs. The footsteps continued. He walked slowly upstairs shining his phone flashlight into the darkness of the house.

"Hannah?" He quivered as he reached the top of the staircase.

A faint voice whispered back from the bedroom behind him, "*Still-well.*"

He swiftly turned around shining the light in the room. It was bare; the curtains were swaying. There was no one there. He crept into the room, shining his light in every corner.

"Who are you?" he asked.

A light caught his eye. It was emanating from the backyard by the well. He approached the window and realized this was the room where he saw the something from the well. He looked at the well, and in full form, practically glowing in the dark, was a white figure looking back up at him. It was about five feet tall with transparent legs and torso. Hovering in midair, it held out supple arms and pointed down the well. The apparition looked back up at Paul, its eyes bleak empty pools of despair. He backed away from the window. "No, no, no..." He heard a heart-wrenching howl, watching stupefied as it flew up to the window, reaching for him.

He screamed as loud as he could, jetting out of the house like a star quarterback. He stumbled back to his car. "Why is this happening?" he screamed. He looked at the house, still in the night. No light, no sign of any ghostly apparitions. His head hurt, a sob escaped his mouth, and he knew he was insane.

***

He sat slumped in the car and reached for his phone but couldn't bring himself to call anyone. He felt alone, a speck of wounded humanity, a dot on the backside of life. His breath escaped, as a light shined into the car.

He saw a black leather knuckle tap his window. Giddy with relief he lowered it to stare into the eyes of a local cop.

"License and registration—hey." The cop looked at his face. "You're Paul Russo. I recognize you from the realtor signs."

"Um...yes. I'm really glad to see you."

"I'll bet. The ghost scare you?"

"What?"

"Oh, we get reports all the time. Caught a few kids here last fall. Scared the shit outta me." He laughed. He watched Paul's white face. "It's just kids. No such things as ghosts, Mr. Russo."

"I know. I was checking on the house."

"Yeah. They do the same thing down at the Randle estate as well as Bingham House." He leaned against the door, confiding. "It's the kids of one of the wealthiest families in the area. We're supposed to scare 'em off. We were warned not to take them in. Politics. Fucking rich bastards."

"I know what you mean. So, they've been doing this for a while?"

"Years."

"Whew. Thought I was going nuts."

"Ha. Just a couple of brats."

"Thanks. Well, I got to get home." He started the car, but his hands still shook.

The officer patted the roof. "Drive safe."

He arrived home. He was exhausted as he saw his parents out. The kids were sleeping the sleep of the just; he checked on each one of them. Jesse's covers were on the floor, Veronica was wrapped in her mother's shawl, and lastly he unplugged Stella's thumb from her pouting lips. It was Thursday. He rubbed both eyes with the heels of his hands. Sleep called to him, but he had to fill out forms for the open house they were having tomorrow. It was the brokers' open house to introduce the Stillwell house. He had a meeting with a couple that was divorcing to price out their home, the first day of dance—a surprise for the girls—and finally Friday night was Molly's psychic party. On top of that, Saturday morning was the first game of basketball for Jesse, and he knew they had to get a report on the state of Nevada done before Monday. Stella had a reading assignment, and lastly, he had to start a science project with Roni. He hadn't done a science project in over twenty years. He didn't know where to begin.

He kicked off his shoes and stared at the TV, thoughts running like squirrels through his head. How was he going to get everything done and still make a living? He thought back to his panicked escape from Stillwell. Man, was he relieved. It was only kids. They were clever; he had to give them that. But that didn't explain the hairy friend who visited him nightly in his sleep. His thoughts called out to him as fatigue consumed him.

He didn't realize he had dozed off until the dream came. It wasn't fair. He was so tired and wasn't even in bed, but it still came. He was standing in his childhood home. It was a split-level in Long Island. The house was fully furnished. He walked upstairs to his old bedroom. Allison used to come over and they played with his toys in there.

The room was spotless. His bed was perfectly made, and Candy Land was tucked away on his shelf along with all the other games they played together. He had model homes he used to love to build and displayed them on his dresser. Legos were piled on a shelf. He'd have to fix that, he thought to himself. They belonged in a box. In Paul's well-ordered world, everything belonged in a box. He walked over and marveled at the small homes. Each was fully decorated with tiny furniture. These were girls' toys, which didn't belong here. This meant Allison was nearby. He smiled but then smelled something awful. Almost rotten. He heard it before he actually saw it hunched on his bed, on all fours. He caught a glimpse of something dark, foul, and hairy. It clawed his comforter, and cotton batting floated around the room. He felt lifted as though he was being propelled to the heavens. Allison floated into his view. She was young, dressed as Alice in Wonderland, her blonde pigtails neatly at her sides.

"Allison." He reached out to her.

She started falling. He tried to follow her but was held back. His shirt was taut against his body, the thing at his back, holding him. He grabbed at the air, trying to turn to swat the ape, but he couldn't. Vile laughter filled the silence.

"Allison, what is happening?" He heard his own boyhood scream as he watched her being sucked into a tunnel.

He started gliding to her, rancid breath moistly blowing on his cheek. Chills ran down his neck. Turning, he tried to see the hairy face, but his eyes were glued shut. His stomach shot acid up his throat. His heart beat frantically against the walls of his chest; it felt like a trapped butterfly. The monster's sibilant growl filled the void. "*Mine*" it repeated until Paul covered his ears to drown out all sound except for his own sobs.

He jumped up to an empty room, the television screen flashing the test sign. It was cold. Shivering, he walked to his bed, his eyes watchful and wary. He stripped and threw himself on the bed, tired, but afraid to sleep. "Ally," he whispered. "I wish I could help you."

CHAPTER SIX
Friday

Morning came with relentless rain. An autumn chill made him put the heat on in the house, and he wondered briefly when he had to order oil. Did it come by itself, or did Allison order the tanks to be filled? He just didn't know. His mother had graciously made lunches, which pleased both him and the children. They left cheerfully with all kinds of sweet surprises in their brown paper bags.

No cleaning woman today, so he did a quick load of laundry and enjoyed the convenience and wonder of grocery home delivery. As he walked the aisles of his cyber store, he realized he better learn to shop with a list, because the bill was astronomical.

He knew he bought too much but arranged the delivery on the day when the cleaning woman could put it away. Let her deal with the mess.

He called Molly, and they organized who was getting what. She placed an order for mini-cobblers at the local inn that had authentic colonial-style cakes. He had suggested they serve tea, since it was a Loyalist house; however, his patriotic friend wouldn't have it.

The brokers' open house was scheduled for ten o'clock. He had arranged for bouquets to be delivered to put in several rooms of the house.

"Did you get the brochures from the printer?" he asked.

"They're in my backseat. The photo's been fixed and our friend is missing from the pictures."

"Yeah, right. I still say it's a trick of light or something."

"Okaaaay," Molly answered. "We'll see what Georgia has to say about that."

***

He drove down 25A and placed signs strategically where people would see them. By the time he got to the house, Molly was inside the kitchen, warming apple turnovers.

"I smell cinnamon, and what is that, cloves? Where's the vanilla?"

"Colonial, Paul. We go with what was available three hundred years ago."

"Have you been upstairs yet?" he asked her, and she understood exactly what he was talking about.

"No, and I'm not going up there alone."

"I'm surprised at you. I met a cop here yesterday; he told me the kids play tricks at night. It's just kids,

Molly. Nothing more than some nasty tricks. Like on Halloween."

"I don't like this place. I wish we could have done the cleansing before the open house."

"It's just the brokers' open. We'll do it before the weekend before the buyers come. We just didn't have enough time this week."

"There should always be enough time for a cleansing." She took a bite out of a steaming pastry. "Yum. Try one. These are delicious."

He beckoned her to the steps and she followed him up the stairs. "This place is plain spooky. No pun intended. I want it gone before Halloween. I am not coming here on October thirty-first."

"I'll get it sold," he said a bit too confidently. They walked toward the last bedroom.

"That's the room?" she asked.

He shook his head.

"I don't like it here." She backed away. "There is an overwhelming sadness. I want to go downstairs. I don't like it here."

He took her hand. "Come on. I'm with you." He opened the door, her hand in his. The door swung open slowly, and they both shivered involuntarily. "It's nothing. Come on."

Hand in hand, they entered the room. The air felt thick, and they both noticed the fragile draperies move. "There is no fucking breeze in here. I am totally freaked out."

"Molly, do you see anything? I don't." He pointed to the empty room. "It's all imagination. It has to be."

In the distance a door slammed and they both jumped. Their eyes met and they rushed out of the room, laughing nervously all the way downstairs.

***

They had a few curious realtors, but overall it was a dismal showing. The rain might have kept people away, but Paul was more than a little nervous he would have trouble selling the house.

After cleaning up the kitchen, he heard Molly shout, "Paul, come here, you've got to see this!" He put down the trash and walked into the main hall.

"Were the flowers fresh?"

"I got them this morning at Bliss, why?"

She moved away so he could see his floral arrangement. This morning he had placed a large glass vase filled with hydrangeas, Gerber daisies, and roses in vibrant shades of purple, pinks, and yellow. Before him was a wilted display, the flowers dried and dying.

"That's strange." He ran into the other rooms. All of the fresh bouquets he had purchased were brown and dead.

"This place gives me the creeps. Let's get out of here."

"You go ahead. I'll finish cleaning up."

"Leave with me. I don't like the feel of this place."

"Just your imagination, Molly. I'll meet you at the Stevens place. We have to give them an eval of what their house is worth."

"See you in…"

"Forty-five."

She left, and he finished tidying up the house. He dumped the flowers and locked the door. He walked around the back then went to the wishing well, wondering if he could make out what he saw the other night.

The sky had cleared, but it still threatened rain. Trees wept with moisture, and soon, his expensive Italian loafers were soaked. Allison would kill him if she saw them. He smiled at that.

The well had two weeping willows draping over it dramatically. He noticed it was quiet; he couldn't hear any birds chirping. He leaned over and peered down the deep hole. Dank moisture met his face. It was humid with the odor of wet moss. Standing on his toes, he squinted in the darkness. There toward the bottom a shiny thing flickered at him. It wasn't copper but gold in color. Embedded in the wall, he couldn't tell if it was a coin, but it appeared smooth and circular. It was too far to reach, so he looked around for something. He spied a branch nearby and picked it up and extended his arm into the well. He reached and stretched farther. He leaned completely over the well, feet planted in the ground.

The heavy limb was weighing him, and for a second, he felt his feet lift off, and he thought he might topple in. Another centimeter and he would have tipped into the well. He heaved himself back onto the wet grass then fell on his ass. Throwing away the branch, he retreated, the glow of whatever was buried in the well winking in his memory.

***

They met at the next stop, a sad and somber affair. Both spouses were there, the hostility so present, the tension in the air could be cut with a knife. Molly's false joviality stood out like a peacock among the pigeons, and he almost told her to shut up already. She was as uncomfortable as he. It was never easy to handle a divorce sale. The house reeked of the bitter root of failure, the oppressive air of anger. Mr. Stevens, a local lawyer, stood by the large picture windows facing a rolling lawn. Mrs. Stevens, who insisted everyone call her "Mariah," sat defeated on a brown velvet love seat, her face forlorn.

Every so often he caught her staring at the indifferent back of her impeccably dressed husband. When he delivered the sad news that they would be "underwater" and get less than what they owed on the mortgage, the husband shrugged coldly, and the wife bit back a sob.

Contracts signed, he vowed to get as much as he could and he meant it. This house had no specters, but it didn't relieve the sadness he felt inside its rooms.

Molly and he left the house and walked toward their cars. "You want pizza tonight?"

"No time. I have a ton of things to do."

"You're coming, right?" she asked nervously.

"I said I would. I have to get the girls for dance class. We have to start a report and I want to be home to feed them. Is eight o'clock OK?"

"I'll feed Georgia. When you get there, you get there. Ciao." She waved her long fingernails at him and dashed off to her convertible.

***

Paul made it home in time to get a nice pot of pasta going. As he chopped vegetables, he wondered if Allison was laughing her cosmic ass off. Using frozen gravy his mom left, he paused remembering how he explained what gravy was to his wife.

"It's red, Paul. It's a sauce." She pointed to the fusilli on her plate covered with her mother-in-law's delicious sauce.

Smiling, he brushed an eyelash from her peach-tinted, freckled cheek. "Gravy. We call it gravy."

"Gravy is brown and you put it on potatoes."

"Only in your Waspy home. This here is some genuine gravy by Arlene Russo."

Laughing, they dug into their pasta dinner.

Lost in thought, he was startled as the first of his brood bustled through the door.

"Stella Luna, go wash and let's get homework out of the way fast!" he ordered.

She ran through the room, dropping her schoolbag at his feet and grabbing a cookie before she rushed away. He tripped over her backpack, cursed, and called after her.

"I'll be right back," she hollered back, and he heard the bathroom door slam.

The twins sauntered in, faces wind kissed and talking in that strange kind of singular conversation only they had. They each took a spot at the table, and Paul explained how the rest of the evening was going to proceed.

"We are doing homework first."

"Oh Dad," Jesse interrupted him. "It's the weekend. Mom gave us Friday evenings off."

"Yeah, but we are kind of behind."

"Have a little faith in us, Dad. We will get to the work, I promise. We need a break too."

"But Stella's got the Nevada report, you have the science fair, and I don't even remember what Jesse has to do."

"Aunt Lisa is coming tomorrow. She can help with the science report, and we'll both help Stella with Nevada."

"I did that report six years ago. I know exactly what to do," Jesse offered.

Well, that was easy, Paul thought. "In any case, we have one hour and then I have a surprise for the girls."

"What is it?" Roni nibbled on the cut-up carrots he placed on the table. He had taken the cookies and put them back into the cabinet.

Veronica went to a blackboard in the corner of the kitchen. "Let's put our assignments up here, and..."

Jesse finished the statement. "Next to it, report where you are up to. I'll put Stella's work up, so you'll know what has to be done."

Paul was impressed with their ingenuity. They were bright kids.

Stella returned to the kitchen and Paul gave them the bag from the dance store. "Go get ready." He smiled at them then he turned to his son. "While they're in class, we'll go get haircuts. How's that?"

"Sounds good. My hair's getting pretty long."

***

They pulled up to a dance studio in the strip mall. He eyed the line of restaurants and noticed it was flanked by a pizzeria, deli, and take-out Chinese. Well, he thought, next week we go international. No more cooking on Friday nights.

He sent Jesse to the barber at the corner and told him to get in line and he would be there shortly. He needed to fill out paperwork for the girls. The front room was empty, and he listened to the excited chatter of his daughters as they hung up the black-and-pink nylon bags he had purchased. Stella was a plump little fairy, round and dimpled in her pink tights and black leotard. Alarmed, he noticed budding breasts on his older daughter to go with her willowy figure. He didn't like that, no sir, he didn't like that at all.

The room started to fill with overweight mommies holding bags for rambunctious, as well as noisy, little girls. The room became animated as his daughters reacquainted themselves with children he didn't know. He thought he was familiar with most of their friends, but it appeared there was a whole world of things he didn't know about his children. A tiny elf-like woman approached him. Black hair pulled back in a tight bun, her dancer duck-like walk had an elegance and he blushed when she caught him staring at her slim calves. Holding out a small hand, she smiled and said, "Mr. Russo..."

"Please, call me Paul."

"Thanks, I'm Ellie Marcus. I own Gotta Dance. I'm so sorry about your wife. She was a great mom."

"And a great wife too, thanks."

"I knew her from LH Wagner," she referred to Stella's elementary school. "My son is in the same second grade class as your daughter. Mrs. Lustig. They both have Mrs. Lustig."

"Oh. Right."

Ellie smiled sweetly. She was a few years younger than him, and as he studied her face, he asked, "Have we met?" She wore tight leggings that hugged her body, and a barely there sleeveless tee that showed off firm arms.

"Well, yes. You got me an apartment about five years ago when I split with my husband."

"Right, your name was different."

"I used my married name then. Marcus is my maiden name."

"It's the girls' first time out since Allison passed."

"I'm glad you brought them in. They've been missed."

He reached for the chain around his neck and felt for the ring under his shirt. Absently, he patted it.

They watched the group of girls split off into different classrooms. "It's show time. See you in an hour."

Paul met his son who was already in the barber chair. They got haircuts at the same time. The barber winked at Paul and lathered up Jesse's face, pretending he was going to shave him with a razor he had sharpened on his leather stop. This brought on chuckles and a momentary pang to Paul's gut. Allison was never going to see their son shave. It put a damper on the whole afternoon for him. He missed her so much. Trying not to show his depression, he picked up the girls and listened to the delightful recounting of dance class.

***

His mother came into the house, loaded with yet more dishes of prepared food.

"I cooked already," Paul told her with a touch of pride.

"What? What did you cook?"

"Rigatoni."

"Rigatoni?" she repeated, shocked. "With what?"

"Your gravy, asparagus, and a salad."

His mother pinched his cheek and told him he made her proud. He felt like a five-year-old. Then she sat down with her grandchildren to hear stories of their day, while they ate their dinner.

He picked up his phone and keys and paused by the door. "Thanks, Ma."

"For what. Get out of here." She waved at him. "Go on...Get outta here. We want to start having fun."

The kids heartily agreed.

***

Paul drove the four miles to Molly's and noticed a white Escalade parked in the driveway. He knocked and Molly let him into the house with her usual warm welcome.

"Georgia's reading my cards. Come sit down and listen."

Half-empty wine glasses sat on the table where a slightly crushed pizza box lay abandoned and empty. They ate a whole pizza. He raised his eyebrows.

A small woman, her hair shocking white in the front and jet black in the rear, sat on the floor in front of Molly's coffee table, tarot cards laid out before her. She turned up her coal black eyes, and he felt unnerved by her direct stare.

"Hi," he said simply.

"Georgie, this is my *friend*, Paul. I'm not going to tell you anything else."

Georgia studied him, her keen eyes taking everything in. He took off his shoes, since Molly didn't allow them in the house, and sat on the couch and told them to finish the reading.

She had a bad complexion, he noted, and wore very tight clothing that showed off a slightly dumpy figure. He guessed being a psychic she didn't need a mirror. She knew what everybody was thinking of her appearance, he thought sarcastically.

She looked up to study his face, and a blush stole up his collar. A feeling of violation overcame him, and for a moment, he considered that she knew exactly what he was thinking. He normally was not rude, but he had to admit, he was off and had been for the last six months.

"Cut the deck again." She was chewing gum and now looked at the three cards on the surface of the table. She had a high-pitched voice that could grate potatoes, Paul thought. No wonder she didn't have trouble; it was certainly a sound that could wake the dead. He smiled to himself.

Georgia zoomed her eyes to meet his and lowered her voice an octave. Maybe she's a mind reader; he smirked.

Molly turned over the first card, interrupting his thoughts. "What does that mean?"

"It's the world. It means fulfillment."

"Well, fulfillment's not bad."

Georgia shrugged. "It's upside down. It means something is not going to be fulfilled. Pick the next one."

"Ah, the two of wands."

"Wands."

"You're successful. You are going to make money. You have a good business sense."

He rolled his eyes and caught Georgia looking at him with an odd smile.

"Three of swords." She placed a stubby hand painted with purple nail polish on Molly.

"That thing you asked me. Not going to happen. Do you understand, not ever."

Molly sighed sadly. "Got it." She rose to her feet. "Are you ready, Paul?"

"Sure. How much does she know about me?"

"Nothing," Molly answered, her face shocked. "I wanted this to be a true reading for you."

"Where do you want me to sit?" He wanted to leave; he didn't believe and felt faintly foolish.

"Let's move to the kitchen table." Georgia got up and went toward the tiny dining table in the kitchen. She gestured for Paul to sit opposite of her. "Don't say anything but yes or no. Don't explain anything to me. Please don't interrupt the reading with a question." Taking out a rosary, she made a brief prayer to a saint he had never heard of. Her eyes fluttered and she took a pad she had placed next to her, scribbling strangely.

"A female presence has entered the room. She could be your sister, sister-in-law, or wife. She is a contemporary of yours. She's calling out for her hero. Oh, oh, you are her hero. Do you understand that? Hero and honey. Honey, she's showing me honey, like in a jar...Is this your wife?"

He nodded, watching her warily.

"You were together a long time, a long time." She looked surprised. "But how could you have been? She passed young, relatively young for today's standards. Yes, she passed young. You look young, but I feel like you were together for like forty years or something. Yes, she's saying you were together for thirty-three, thirty-four years, but that makes no sense."

It made sense to Paul, who had known Ally since they had been in diapers.

"You had an apple pie household; it was a happy household. You know what I mean. You were happy. She was happy." Here Georgia touched her head. "A stroke?" She cocked her weird-colored head. "Cancer?" Her lips moved, but no sound came out. "She had a brain tumor. There was nothing you could do. It was fast. It was horrible, what they did to her. It was too much, like they tried to save her, but couldn't. She wants to thank you for taking good care of her."

He bit back a sob, swallowing and clearing his throat. It was her voice but not her voice. It was strange. He was sitting with this woman but hearing his wife. The expressions, the way she moved her head. It was Allison. Totally absorbed, he drank in the presence. He wanted more. Serenity filled him until the only thing that existed was Georgia and Paul, or in his mind, Allison and Paul.

She continued, "She had a rough passing. Wait… Wait…She's calling out to children. The number three is predominant. Do you take three? Two of one kind, one of the other. She's showing me Gemini. Do you have twins? She's laughing. One of them is like the spawn of Satan. A hell-raiser but a good boy, really. He gives you a run for the money, huh?" Here she paused and cocked her head as if listening. "Does the month of June have meaning for you?"

He shook his head. "No."

"She keeps saying 'June.' I'll leave that with you."

"She's showing me movies. I see cowboys, no, they're outlaws. Jesse James. Huh."

He gasped, realizing that June was her mom and not the month, and Ally was calling out for their son. He touched the ring resting against his chest.

"She's showing me the stars and the moon. Do you understand that? She says you'll understand that. She's laughing. She says you're being dense today."

A tear trickled down his cheek, and Molly ran from the room with a sob.

"You know the story of when Christ was walking with the cross? She showed it to me. Do you know that story? You know, he sweating and Veronica gives him a towel and he wipes his face on it. I don't know what she means, but she says you'll understand. Does it mean something to you? Either the story or the name?"

"Yes," he whispered. "I understand."

"She's a free spirit. Kind. She was happy here. You made her happy. You had a good life together. Short," Georgia said wistfully, "but that's the way of it. She's showing me Alice in Wonderland. She says it's her in the blue dress. Was she blonde? Is that what she's trying to convey? Wait, don't answer." Her eyes were closed. "Yes, yes...She's talking about a monkey."

He froze.

"Yes, a monkey wrench." The black eyes came up and bore into his. "There's a monkey wrench she is complaining about."

"I...I don't know. I don't know what you are talking about." He sat forward.

"Well..." Georgia laughed. "Neither do I, honey. She's showing me a big hairy ape and saying 'monkey wrench' and she's insisting that you would recognize it."

He couldn't stop the gasp that escaped his throat.

"Did you lose a child?"

"No!" he shouted. "Wait, go back to the monkey!"

Georgia ignored him. "You did lose a child. She's telling me she's with your child." Again she cocked her head. "It was never born, a miscarriage. Your wife had a miscarriage."

"Four years ago." He was shocked. No one but their parents knew about that.

"Oh, she's saying, 'make the kids eat vegetables.' Ha ha. Wait. She's telling me to tell you that dancing will be good for all of you. She's showing me sugarplum fairies, you know, like at the ballet. She's pulling back now."

He sat on the edge of his seat. "Wait."

"She says to watch for a ring. You need to find a ring."

A ring, he thought wildly. He placed his hand on her wedding band on the chain around his neck once again.

"Not her wedding band." She paused. "She knows you wear her ring close to your heart. You'll know which ring when you find it. She loved you. Oh my." Georgia touched her cheek, her dark eyes glistening with tears. "She loved you so much. More than eternity."

He fingered the ring. They had engraved their rings with the quote "More than eternity" on the outside of both bands. It was their own private thing. He used to ask her how much she loved him and she always replied, "More than eternity." This shook Paul's insides.

"Whew." Georgia pulled herself out of her communication. "I do a lot of readings. Your wife loved you, man. Really loved you. It was a pleasure." She held out her hand to him. "And she knew you loved her back just as much. It was a pleasure reading you."

"Is she OK?" he asked softly, still not believing what had just happened.

"I...There's a monkey wrench. That's all I can say. Once everything gets sorted out, I think you'll know more," she added cryptically.

Molly showed Georgia out of the house and turned to him. "So what did you think?"

"Well, it was interesting. She's a character. Did you tell her anything about my life?"

"No, no, and no. And did I say no? Do you feel better?"

He winced. "I have unanswered questions. That was certainly amazing. Interesting. If she's for real, it was profound. But," he added, "I feel I have to help Ally in some way."

"I booked her to do a cleansing at the house tomorrow before the open house. She'll be there at eleven, if you're interested."

"I'll be there."

He left Molly's unsatisfied, and the car somehow took him to Stillwell. He parked in the drive and got out and walked toward the terrace. It had gotten cold; puffs of condensation swirled around his head from his breathing. It was quiet, no sounds, darker than Hades, he thought. Purple clouds parted revealing a brilliant harvest moon, its orange light bathed the landscape so that it glowed. He stood on the terrace and looked out across the expanse of the lawn to the well. Two orbs danced above the opening. He knew it would be too long to run down there to see what was happening. He fumbled for his camera phone and tried to take a picture. They froze with the flash of his camera, dipping into the well, only to bounce up and spin toward him. They raced past him, and he felt the air stir as they grazed his cheeks. Touching his face, his fingers wet, it was damp with his own tears. He knew this was not the work of teenagers.

***

"I'm glad you took the girls to dance," his mother told him over a cup of tea they shared later that night. "You have to start living again."

He sighed. "Ma...I..." He was jumpy, on edge. He was afraid of what he was thinking. Fear ruled him. If anyone knew what was going through his mind, they'd take the kids away. His logical self couldn't believe what Georgia had told him, and he considered that Molly unwittingly gave out his story.

"I'm not saying to join eHarmony today but Paul. I know you loved Ally, we all did, but you're a young man."

"I'm not interested. Would you go out with someone if something happened to Pop?"

"God forbid." She paused. "It's no good to be alone."

He patted her hand and they sat in silence for a while. He was wrestling with so many things. Thoughts swirled in his brain. Monkey wrench, Alice in Wonderland, orbs in the night, Hannah Andrews, but Paul confided to his mom the only thing he was absolutely sure about. "Ma," he said and looked into her brown eyes. "Veronica needs a bra."

141

His mother promised to handle that for him and asked if he had prepared her for getting her period, to which she was treated to a panicked response that threatened to wake the kids. She assured him she'd help with that too. Looking at his white face, she urged her son to get a good night's sleep and make sure he had bicarbonate soda before bed. It was good for his digestion.

He slid between the sheets, thinking and replaying his session with Georgia, wondering what she meant by the monkey wrench. In a way, it had been satisfying. She knew the kids' names, remembered certain things about their relationship, and when she mentioned the lack of vegetables in their diet, he damn near shit in his pants. Molly couldn't have known about that. What about their wedding bands? Who even knew that about them? Could the fact she quoted what was engraved on their rings be a coincidence? He fell asleep, Georgia's reading still in his ears.

The corridor was back. The mist was thicker, Allison's cries more distinct. The roar of that thing, that hairy beast echoed on the stark walls. Paul was running, his shirt stuck to his back, and his shoulders bounced against the walls, slowing him. Allison was in the distance; he reached out for her. The ape-like tail grabbed his wrist. The thing pulled and dragged him. His own nails scored the walls, trying to find something to hold onto. He was being pulled downward, the walls getting closer together, until, it looked more like a tube. As he braced his shoulders against the narrowing passage, he pulled back, fighting the demon, trying to escape. Allison's voice echoed in his head. He heard her repeating, "Monkey wrench..."

He felt the chain being ripped from his neck. Suddenly, he awoke and felt around his soft sheets, his hand finding a broken chain and the ring under his pillow.

CHAPTER SEVEN
Saturday

The next day dawned clear, and Paul felt anything but bright as he looked at his bleary face in the mirror. It was early. The day was overcast with the promise of rain. "Great," Paul thought wearily anticipating a glum open house. Jesse was going to basketball practice this morning after breakfast. He got the kids up and dressed with a promise of many surprises. They left without eating, and when they pulled into the diner, they squealed with delight. He hadn't taken them out to eat from the time Allison first got sick. She had been so nauseous that food had to be eaten where she could reach a bed and a bathroom quickly. A feast of scrambled eggs and pancakes was enjoyed. He allowed Veronica to have a very light cup of coffee. Her twin was still content with juice. He smiled at his children, enjoying the fresh-faced coloring. Jesse's anger had slowly dissipated, Veronica seemed more at ease, and baby Stella was, well, still baby Stella.

He stopped in at the jeweler who repaired his chain, and he felt whole as he slipped it back over his head.

"Looks like someone ripped it off your neck." The jeweler showed him twisted links he was replacing. "Sorry about your wife. I...hate to ask you, but you were supposed to pick this up a few months ago."

The older man brought out a pouch with a bracelet with all the kids' names on it on small round coins. Paul's heart twisted in his chest.

"Sorry, I forgot. It was for Christmas. How much do I owe you?"

The man considered him. "I hate to make you pay, but I can't do anything because they are engraved. You know they're specific to your family."

"I understand. Don't worry about it." Paul pulled out his charge card, paying the balance. The girls stood on tiptoes wanting to see, but he put the small bag in his jacket pocket.

"What is it?"

"Nothing. It's nothing," he murmured as they departed the store.

He dropped Jesse at the school for practice then drove the girls to a local nail salon that he knew Allison had frequented. He got out of the car and took both their hands and took his happily skipping children for a mani pedi. The Asian ladies in the salon talked him into having one as well, so he sat with his pants rolled high between his daughters drifting pleasantly as his feet were massaged into putty.

He was fine until he noticed that they were taking the tools from a small personalized kit. It lay on the floor being used by his family. The kit had Allison's name on it.

Time to go again, and while his tense muscles had been pummeled while the girls got polish, he knew the hard knots were back, tying up his shoulders.

Lisa was waiting when they got home, ready to enter science fair hell with his daughter. She started to explain the project, but Paul raised his hand to stop her. "Did I say thanks, no? Well, thank you from the bottom of my heart. And if you are so inclined for sainthood, could you help Stella with her Nevada report?"

Lisa smiled at him and walked him to the door. "There will be a price, little brother." She whispered as they reached the door, "You're looking better." Her eyes appraised him.

"Wow. Have I got a story for you."

She looked at him curiously, "I'm all ears."

"I need about two hundred years to tell it. It's nuts."

Hugging him, she said, "Well, I'm just happy you seem to be more like yourself."

He shuddered and wondered if everyone was blind.

***

He got to Stillwell Manor early, just before the caterer. Trays of tea sandwiches were brought in. College kids in white jackets set up hors d'oeuvre trays, and a tea and coffee station was prepared in the kitchen. Georgia came early, Molly in the car behind him.

"Nice digs." Georgia eyed the double-floored entry. "Gives me the willies, though." She shivered.

Well, thought Paul, that wasn't encouraging. He smiled and said, "Let's get this thing going." He looked at Molly. "Before people start arriving."

"I think we have a bit of company already." Georgia's dark eyes scanned the high ceilings as she pulled out a huge clam shell. She put it on the kitchen table and opened a plastic bag and took out a bag filled with herbs. He rolled his eyes and hoped it wouldn't conflict with Molly's cinnamon buns toasting in the oven.

Georgia lit the small offering and started waving the scented smoke with her hands. "This place is full of it." She turned to Paul and said, "But you knew that already."

Walking from room to room, the smoke formed a line like a heat-seeking missile looking for spirits.

It took a half hour to finish the downstairs, and as they climbed the grand staircase, Georgia stopped dead in her tracks. "This isn't going to be enough."

She turned to Paul, her eyes wide. "This has never happened before. It's not going to be enough. I don't know what to do." As if drawn by a magnet, they climbed up the stairs and she moved unerringly to the last bedroom.

"She's here. Oh...She's so sad. She's waiting for her... Oh, oh, oh." Georgia's eyes filled with tears, her voice heavy with sorrow. "Nobody understands what happened, and this has made her so unhappy. I have never seen such sorrow." Her voice was a nasal whine.

"What?" Paul demanded. "What do you see?"

"What's happening now?" Molly asked.

"She won't hurt you. She's waiting and she won't leave until she gets what she wants."

"Well, that don't sound too good. If she didn't get it in two hundred forty years, chances are it's not gonna happen. Can you tell her?" Molly snorted.

"She knows, but it doesn't matter. There's a monkey wrench."

"Stop saying that!" Paul yelled.

"I can't help it. I say what they are telling me."

"There is nothing I can do about that damn monkey wrench." He was shouting now, clearly at the end of his rope. "I think we've had enough of this nonsense."

Georgia looked at him, her face serene. "Hannah says you'll get all your answers when you look up."

"Look up? Where? Where? I don't understand."

"You will." Georgia blew out the smoldering sage and left the house.

"That was a crock of shit."

"Well, I believe," Molly said.

Minutes later Melissa and Craig came by. "Did your psychic exorcise the house?" Craig asked blandly.

Paul shrugged and Melissa laughed. "I didn't know you became a spiritualist."

"I'm not." Suddenly he was tired of Melissa and Craig and their house of drama. He wanted to be done with this venture.

"What's your lowest number?"

"20.8 and they can have it lock, stock, and barrel."

It was a good price. Paul vowed to work his ass off to get rid of it. He glanced out in the yard and saw a flash of light over the well. "Did you see that?" he asked Craig.

"What?"

"A flash of light."

"I thought you had the house cleaned of its spirits," Craig said.

"Maybe they left the house and are waiting for you to leave so they can come back," Melissa said. "Let's get out of here. I've had enough of this place."

They left much to Paul's relief. It was always easier to show a home without its owners. He glanced around and said loudly, "Even the dead ones."

As the morning progressed, crowds of people arrived. Many were curious about the house and wanted to see what it looked like inside. Others were interested in seeing if they could make a steal. They had over a hundred leads by the time they removed the signs by two o'clock. Paul locked up and both he and Molly were happy to quit the place an hour later. He did have one interested party. They made a first-time bid of 19.8 million, and he knew he could probably get them up. They were Wall Street money, buckets of it. A young couple, who was talking architects already, was in love with its "charm." He could tell them a thing or two about the charm. It would be an amazing coup, a huge payoff for both him and Molly that would put his finances back where they used to be. His chest swelled with the thought that with everything that had occurred, he hadn't lost his ability to sell. It was after five and he wanted to get out of the place.

***

Heading home, he stopped to pick up pizzas for the kids and walked into a kitchen where papers were strewn all over the table, books lay open on the counter, and a beaker let off steam by the sink. It was pandemonium; somehow it felt good.

"What's going on in here?" He put the pizza on a chair, the only bare surface.

"Let me see your nails, Paul. The girls tell me you got a mani pedi today," his sister teased him. "Takes a real man to sit through that," she whispered into his ear with a chuckle.

"I appreciate that, sis. I brought pizza."

"Great. I'm starved."

Together, they helped the kids get everything organized and put away to finish by tomorrow. They ate while the television blared, the lights were overly bright, and the kitchen had an overall festive feeling. He cleaned up the paper plates then let the kids watch one last program before bed. He was sitting in comfortable silence with his sister in the kitchen. Fingering the chain around his neck, he started to relate his evening with Georgia.

"Sounds unreal. I mean she *did* know some good stuff. The twins, the kids' names. Your ring. It's a lot," his sister offered, her large hands wrapped around a mug of tea.

"One side of me wants to believe so badly, but there's this other side. You know, like the scientific...logical side. It's hard to suspend belief."

"But Paul...She knew so much. June's name. What's the monkey wrench about? What was she talking about?"

151

He turned his head not answering.

"Paulie. What's up with the monkey business?"

"I...I've been having dreams." He kept his voice low. "Since the funeral. Jesse had the same dream. It's like she's being held captive by this ape thing," he added in a whisper, "a demon."

Lisa crossed herself. "Stop. What are you talking about? It's just your grief. Have you talked to anybody?"

"Who am I gonna talk to? You make me feel like a mental patient. Who am I gonna tell a demon has Allison? They're gonna take my kids away."

"You should talk to a shrink. This is too much. You have to talk to someone before you have a breakdown. You should take Jesse."

He shook his head. "He's better. It only happened a few times for him. He hasn't complained in a few days."

"He does seem happier."

He nodded, relieved. "I have to wait this thing out. I know the answers are right in front of me. It's as though there's this strange triangle involving Stillwell, Hannah, Allison, and myself."

"That's a rectangle."

He looked up at her in question.

"You said triangle; that would involve three parties, but you included the house."

"Thank you, Euclid. The scales have fallen from my eyes."

She laughed. "That's my brother. See, it's just the strain, Paul. It's the strain of losing Allison. She was the center of your life."

"She still is," he said quietly.

She started to respond, but his cell rang. It was Molly.

"Hi, Mol. What's the matter?"

"I forgot to close this root cellar door," she told him. "It's too dark for me..."

"Hold on." He turned to his sister. "I have to go back to Stillwell. Do you mind staying with the kids for an hour?"

"It's so dark and it's raining, Paulie, leave it for tomorrow."

"Can't. If an animal crawls in, I'll have to pay for the damage. I gotta go. Can you stay?"

"I'll go with you."

"No, I want to go. Will you watch the kids?"

She shrugged. "Sure."

"I got it, Molly. No, no, it's OK. I don't mind. No, I'm not afraid!" This was said louder than he intended and his kids glanced back at him.

He grabbed his jacket and told them, "Get ready for bed. I'll be back soon."

Stella ran to the large window in the front of the house calling forlornly after him with her face pressed up against the rain specked, living room window, calling, "Daaaaaddy…"

***

It was pitch black outside, the roads covered with rain slicked leaves. He let himself in, scrambled to the basement, and turned on every light he could find. Sure enough the door was open, but he didn't hear the scurry of small feet. He closed the door and raced up the stairs, happy to be done.

As he entered the center hall, ready to leave, he saw an orb dance on the steps. He approached it then held out his hand and watched as the orb caressed him, filling him with both peace and warmth. It danced up and down his arm, his hairs standing up. He felt it beckon him, pull him up the stairs, so he climbed carefully, feeling the tug of the light. The orb floated above him, touching his cheek, leading him to the bedroom. It caressed his face—it was light as a feather—and shined brightly in his eyes, and he saw himself reflected there. The door opened easily; a faint outline stood by the window. She turned, her face flaring with light, her eyes pleading. Pointing down, Hannah urged to him to go to the well. Her ghostly eyes looked upward and his own eyes followed. There was a small door built into the ceiling. It was old, not hinged, almost a cutout that had replaced a hole. "Yeah, just a bunch of kids," he told the apparition. He dragged a chair just below the opening. He used his fingers and tried to pry it open, but it wouldn't budge. He looked down and saw knitting needles in a basket in the corner near the fireplace. Then he used the bone needle as a tool and chipped at the spot until it gave way with an avalanche of dust raining down on him.

He used the chair to lift himself up, his arms straining as his fingers searched the opening. He went into the attic. His fingers came in contact with the frayed binding of a book. With a satisfied sigh, his fingers inched toward it.

It slipped through his sweaty hands then came to rest on the floor. He jumped down, staring at the faded fabric of the cover. He looked up at the window, but his ghostly companion had left. He picked it up and opened it, shining the light of his cell phone on the yellowed pages. The ink had turned brown with age, the pages brittle in his fingers. Gingerly, he leafed through the book. It was a journal, written 235 years ago. It was the private diary of Hannah Andrews. Excited with his find, he put it under his jacket protectively and left for his home.

***

Paul walked in. His sister was at the table doing a jigsaw puzzle. It was spread across the surface, a small section established. He glanced sideways, recognizing St. John's, a historic church in Cold Spring Harbor.

"It's a puzzle of the town."

"Yeah, Allison bought it at the church auction last year. We never got around to doing it."

"You don't mind?"

"What, no. I don't mind at all. Neither would she. You gonna crash here?"

"Do you want me to? What did you find?"

Gently, he pushed the pieces away to make a spot at his end of the table. "Kids?"

"All asleep. You know it's past ten, right?"

He ignored her comment. "Look, it's Hannah Andrews's diary."

"No shit. The murdered girl from Stillwell?"

"The one and only. I found it in a small crawl space over her room. You interested?"

"Sure." She continued with the puzzle.

"She's a young girl here." He scanned the pages. "Hah, she complained about the sermon at St. John's. Wow."

They both looked at the incomplete picture on the table.

"Funny. It's like we're all connected."

Thunder boomed and lightening lit up the window bathing their faces in electric blue. Their eyes met and they laughed, but drew closer together. They heard the rain pummel the roof.

"Tell me about it!" he huffed. "I'm cutting to the chase." He flipped the pages carefully to the year of 1777. "Here." He squinted as he started to read: "I met a boy. He's the son of Mr. Wendover. Mr. Wendover and my father had some business to conduct. His name is John and is as swarthy as a gypsy."

"She's cute," Lisa said. "Get to the good stuff."

"Wait," Paul mumbled, taking it all in. His lips moved rapidly as he read to himself. "The romance progresses. They are meeting by the wishing well, secretly. Her maid, an Irish one…" He looked at her.

"And that is significant, because…" she said without looking up.

"Because June's ancestor was an Irish maid in the household."

"And you know that because?"

"June related a story about her ancestor."

"Yeah, but I'm sure they had more than one Irish maid."

"Could be, but only one left because she was pregnant by the boss. Listen to this: 'I despise my father. Brigitte is increasing. He is a beast. I know it was him. She has not told me, but I have seen her bruises. She is a dear, sweet little thing. He is an animal, a great hairy beast who takes advantage of defenseless servants. Should I tell Mama?'"

"Wow. Now that would make a good book."

"There's more: 'My hatred grows. He has forbidden me from seeing John. I love John. I fear the worst has happened. I am increasing and my father has locked me in my room. What shall I do about my babe? John has promised that we would wed. Papa has forbidden me from seeing him. I will not be able to hide my babe much longer.'"

"Gothic. Keep going."

"'Brigitte has come to me.'" Paul added, "Oh, it's terrible." Then he continued reading: "She has overheard my father's plotting. They are planning on putting compromising papers on John's person. They will hang him as a traitor. My father thinks to end our romance in a heinous way. He is pure evil. I shall die if I can't have my John. Sweet John...my own sweet love, who shall protect us. Who will protect our child? I greatly fear what my father will do. He will give away the babe. I must protect the babe. I must find a way to protect John and our child."

"Do you think the father murdered his own daughter?" Lisa sat back, engrossed in the diary.

"Don't know. She's scribbling here, it's hard to read. I don't quite know what..." He read silently.

"What! Share, Paulie. I'm totally titillated." She hit his arm.

"She's planning an escape. They are going to meet by the well. The date, shit, look at the date." His finger pointed to the date on the top of the yellowed page. It was 235 years ago, tonight.

"Wow. I just got the chills."

"I gotta go back there."

"Paulie," his sister pleaded. "It's enough with that house. It's late. It's pouring."

"Lee. I want to go. I have to go."

"It's not a haunted house. It's haunting you. You're searching for Allison. You have to stop this obsession. It's possessing you."

As if on cue, a crack of thunder shook the house.

"In more ways than you know. I think I'll get the answers tonight. It's too coincidental, the diary, the apparition…"

"What apparition? Paul, this is getting too weird. Maybe, we should…" She reached for the diary.

"I'm not insane, Lisa, I know what I'm seeing. What I am dreaming. It's not kids; it's Allison and she needs me. She's communicating with me. Allison needs me. Please stay here tonight. Let me finish this."

"I'm afraid to think what you need. Maybe some little blue pills." She stared at her brother, worried about him, her face pained.

"I'm not nuts. I'm not crazy. I have to see this through," he told her quietly.

"I'll wait up." His sister held his hand. "Do what you have to do."

"You don't have to wait up." He grabbed his jacket and keys and rushed out the door.

"But I will," she told the empty room.

***

The road was dark. Light pooled only around areas that had lampposts, the road of ribbon a silver, wet and slick. He careened onto 25A; it was empty, not even the cops were out. In the dark distance, the rain made it hard to see. Squinting, he made out a shape, which was a lump, crawling into the middle of the road. His wipers brushed furiously at the downpour and the road lit up as its void was fractured with a jagged bolt of lightning. The lump rose to its feet, holding out both arms to stop him. He swerved, but as he bypassed, he felt a hard thump hit the car. He glanced back, and searched, but could see nothing but stygian darkness. He slowed, feeling his nerves raw, gripping the steering wheel with white knuckled hands. Not more than five feet, it rose up again, now closer to the middle of the hood of his car. It was the beast. Out in the open. He pressed the gas, hoping to hit it. He wanted to see its ugly, hairy face when it died. Adrenaline rushed through his body, he sat up, his face a snarl of rage. He wanted to kill. The engine groaned as he put the gas pedal to the floor, and he heard a resounding crunch as the car drove over the thing. "Come meet me, face to face, you mother fucker!" he screamed at the monster. He turned in his seat and lost control for a minute as the car skidded into an embankment. He got out holding a bloody nose, the rain plastering his shirt to his body, running back to see if it was dead. He jogged ten feet, sloshing through puddles and saw nothing. He searched for a landmark to see where it went down, and couldn't find anything. He looked at his car lying sideways, walked another twenty feet, and saw there was nothing there. His breath came in short pants as he ran back to his car. He ran his hand along the front fender and felt for signs of an impact. There was none. No blood, no hair, no dent. What was happening to him?

He saw through the gloom that he was at the base of the Stillwell driveway. Grabbing the key and his phone, he approached the entrance, lightening flashing and the smell of ozone heavy in the night air.

He pressed on, running up the driveway in the pitch black to Stillwell, the house a dark silhouette in the night sky. It was silent as he opened the front door. His feet echoed in the stark hallways. Taking the steps two at a time, he launched himself upstairs, leaving a trail of water. He positioned himself near the window, gazing out at the well. The orbs were back, dancing around the stone structure.

"Show yourself to me!" he urged. "How does this tie in to Ally?" He felt a tug on his shoulder, and as he turned, a beastly arm swung forward and hit his chin. It tasted salty with blood. It was back! A huge foot stomped his gut, and he rolled impotently on the floor. A well of anger surged within him and he jumped, smacking down the demon, its tail whipping around in a wild frenzy. They rolled on the floor toward the doorway. His knuckles split as he pummeled the hard hairy back of the thing. "Ow, ow, ow." He shook his bruised hand. It hurt like a mother. He kicked the beast hard, satisfied with the hiss of pain. He used the wall to steady himself and rose and scrambled out of the room, a hot breath of hell on his back. The stairs rose up to meet him as the monster landed on his back. They tumbled down together in a bizarre primal dance. He escaped to run out of the house, but for a reason he couldn't explain, he ran to the well instead of the safety of 25A.

The well was lit with an unexplainable incandescence. Paul raced toward the shining beacon while slipping on wet grass. Hot breath heated his shoulder, the dank smell of rot enveloping him. His fingers bit into the solid cobblestone of the well. He leaped onto its wall and reached for the orbs, wanting to grab them. Touch them. He could feel them glide upon the hairs of his arms. Like static electricity, it didn't hurt, but crackled with energy. Their heat enveloped him. Reaching forward, he held out an arm, his balance precarious. The cobblestones were slick with water. A solid thunk to his back sent him reeling downward, his head banging into the hard wall of the dark cavern. Lights flashed behind his eyes; he saw a figure in the distance. He reached out, but the floor rushed up to him and then the air left his body as he hit the bottom of the well.

It was so silent it hurt. Time seemed suspended and he didn't know if it was minutes or hours later. He felt lighter than air and rose slowly upward. Enveloped in peace, he glanced back to see himself lying on the bottom of the well. He was dry, the rain had stopped. Oh, he thought, so this is death. Music came to him, soft whispers of sound, not quite singing, but a peaceful chanting. A light pricked the darkness, growing larger and larger as he moved toward it. A woman dressed in white had her back to him, tendrils of blonde hair swaying around her graceful body. She was surrounded in a white light, so bright it should have hurt his eyes, but strangely it didn't. As he reached out, he noticed his hand showed no sign of his fight; his knuckles weren't bruised or bleeding. "Allison," he whispered, happy and relieved to feel her presence. She held out a translucent hand and turned her palm up to stop him. She floated in one spot. "What..."

"I love you, Paul." Her voice was like music.

He swallowed the lump that lodged in his throat. Her voice continued, "I love you, but you must do something first." He heard her loud and clear, though her lips never moved. "You must deal with the demon first."

He drew back but knew it was behind him. Its hot breath bathed his neck, while rivulets of fear curled down his spine.

"Turn around, Paul, and face your demon. Paul..."

"I don't want to," he pleaded.

"But you must." She shook her head. She gave his shoulder a slight push, and he knew there was no way he could refuse her.

"I'm here to save you," he persisted, trying one last time, suddenly afraid to turn around.

"If you truly want to help me, you have to face the demon...Turn, Paul." Her voice echoed in his mind.

Slowly, he spun, his eyes tightly shut. He could hear the rasping bellows of its breath and smell the decay of its existence. It came close, so close he felt its bared teeth against his cheek.

"Open your eyes, my love."

He slowly opened his eyes to look at the great hairy beast. Though its shoulders were big, and it had the long arms of its monkey ancestor, the face that Paul saw reflected was not a monster. It was not simian but quite human. It was a face he knew oh so well. Staring back was his own image. Grave and wounded, sad and defeated, he looked at himself, the monster within himself.

"You have to let me go," his wife told him gently. He turned, tears gathering in his eyes. "You have to stop fighting. Release me. If you love me, you will let me go." Her voice echoed in his head.

"I can't. I love you. I don't want to, I don't want to," he whispered like a child. "I don't want to be without you. It's me. I am the monkey wrench!" he cried.

"Yes, my dear, my sweet, my own. Your love is holding me back. You have to release me. I need to go."

He swayed, his heart breaking. Sensing his pain, Allison touched his chest, filling him with light and love. "I am right here, Paul." Her hand caressed his chest. "I will always be right here." The electricity pulsed through his heart.

"Our love is eternal and you will never be without me. Release me, Paul. Remember our pledge; it's on our rings.

I will love you more than eternity." He moved toward her, ready to take her hand and go. She slipped out of his grasp, holding up a palm to halt him. "It's not your time now, Paul. You can't go with me. You still have things to do. Yes, I know you want to go, but you can't. I will be waiting for you. I will be the first face you see when we meet again. As long as there are stars in the sky, I will be waiting for you."

Contentment started to replace regret as he watched the monster beside him shrink, slowly disappearing. It deflated, sinking into a smudge, leaving only a soft wisp of smoke.

"It was my time, dear heart. I came to do what I had to do in this lifetime. You have not completed your lessons. Learn quickly, my love, but not too quickly. There are still sunrises for you to enjoy." Soft words caressed his face as he felt Allison around him, inside and out.

"But I don't want…" He heard the words come out as a petulant whine.

His wife became as translucent as smoke, and he watched her brighten once more, only to fade away. A ghostly hand gently touched his cheek, and he knew suddenly that she was gone. Perhaps forever.

Allison's tinkling laughter echoed in his head as he became aware of the aches that consumed his body. Gritty dirt filled his mouth; his skin screamed from a dozen raw places. He heard the incessant ring of his cell phone and realized it was lying outside the well. His sister's cries coupled with the sound of sirens wailing in the background. He cleared his throat, unsuccessfully crying out, "Here!" It came out as a croak, and he wondered how he was going to explain all this. It was daylight, and the rain had stopped. A soggy sun lit the well. He moved his arm, but it was dead weight. Broken, maybe. It rippled with pain as he tried to pull himself up. He was one massive bruise. A glint caught his eye, and he sat up, his back against the stone well. Reaching with his good hand, he pried the gold thing embedded in the rock. It came loose with the struggle and fell to the bottom of the damp well, circling to rest in front of his knee. There was enough light now. As he inched over, he picked up the ring. It had engravings on the inside as well as the outside. He brushed years of dirt and saw the words "more than eternity" engraved on the outside. He pushed himself upright and scanned the inside of the ring. "Hannah and John Married September 1777." He made a fist and clutched it.

A chill danced down his spine, and he watched a rope slither down the well. "You OK, buddy? We're coming down."

"No." He stood slowly. "I'm fine. I didn't see the well and stumbled in. I can get up on my own." He held onto the rope then straightened his arm with a groan. It appeared to work, bruised not broken, after all. He put one foot in front of the other, gripped the rope, and heaved himself up and out of the musty well, his newly awakened muscles screaming in protest.

"I was so worried. I kept calling and calling your phone." His sister brushed at the bruise on his forehead. "What happened? Oh my God, Paulie. I was so scared.

What did you do to yourself?" His sister lovingly checked him for damage.

"Later. I want to go home. I'll tell you later." His voice sounded rusty to his own ears.

"Do you think we should go to the hospital? They want to call the paramedics."

"I'm fine." He stretched. "A bit bruised. Nothing much. Let's get out of here."

An officer approached him. "Was it those kids? Did they push you in? I'll have their hides for this."

"No. Really. I stumbled in."

The officer eyed him.

"One day I'm gonna nail those little bastards."

"I'm sure you will." Paul smiled.

His kids ran to him. They had been corralled by the police on the terrace. Crouching, he gathered them to his chest and kissed their heads. The twins, satisfied he was well, started walking toward their car. Stella held onto his leg. He disengaged her and bent low.

"I'm OK, honey. Let's go home."

"Mommy?" She cocked her head.

"Mommy is fine. Really fine."

Stella smiled sweetly, and when they turned to leave, she pulled him back from the departing people. She tugged his arm and pointed, "Daddy, look!"

The sky was bright with the promise of a new day. He held Stella's hand as two ghostly specters materialized and met face to face. They hovered over the Stillwell wishing well. Hannah and her John stood together, hands clasped like a bride and groom. They turned slowly, their faces peaceful, happy. Hannah touched the slight swell of pregnancy at her waist. She looked up and smiled at Paul then raised her hand and gently waved farewell. Stella waved back. As they turned to the other direction, they floated hand in hand, vanishing into the horizon.

Paul looked down at the ring clasps in his hand, his thoughts on Allison, his children, and love. He considered what people do for love, honor, sacrifice. Closing his hand into a fist, he whispered Allison's last words to him. "As long as there are stars in the sky." He knew for sure she would be waiting for him.

Stella tugged on his hand and he bent painfully to be face to face with her. "Where is Mommy now? Right now?"

He pointed to his chest and then touched hers. "As long as there are stars in the sky, Mommy is right here with us. She will always be with us."

He picked her up and took his older children's hands to live the life they had chosen. To fulfill the dreams of the ages, to complete his job, so that he could reach for the stars someday and be reunited with his Allison.

Epilogue

Stillwell was sold for $20.2 million, an astounding price, considering its reputation. It was lovingly refurbished to all its former glory. Parties, once again, graced its halls and grounds and the Stillwell wishing well was filled with many shiny new coins with happy wishes. Paul never saw Craig or Melissa Andrews again. He heard they sold their house with another agent and divorced shortly after that. Molly continued to be his partner but took another job in the evenings as an assistant to Georgia Oaken. The ghosts of Hannah and John were never seen again.

Paul kept the diary. He felt as though it was a part of him. His house had become peaceful, the ache in his heart healed. He knew now that he felt her love and that though he couldn't see her, she surrounded him, enjoying his small victories at survival.

The summer day dawned bright and clear. They had packed a picnic basket and were planning a day at the shore. The car was filled with happy children, as well as a couple of guests. Ellie Marcus and her son had started joining them more and more as they ventured out in the summer.

He pulled into the gravel driveway of St John's Church. It was high on a hill overlooking a beautiful pond that surrounded it like a green bowl.

"What are we doing here?" Jesse grumbled. "It's not Sunday and this is not our church."

"You're right. I have to look something up." He held out a bag of old bread. "Go feed the ducks in the pond around back." Jesse grabbed the bag, but Paul held it just out of his reach. "No pushing, or shoving, and you two," he said and looked at Jesse and his older twin, "watch the younger ones by the water."

"Gotcha." Jesse grabbed the bag, shouting, "Wait until you see how they all fight over the bread."

The kids scrambled out of the car.

"A church, Paul?" Ellie looked up at him, her eyes bright. They had just started sleeping together. She twined her fingers through his. Ellie waited patiently for him, investing time, listening until one day he noticed her, really noticed her. It was a sweet courtship, and while Ellie knew his first love was Allison, she was more than willing to be his second. He had a rare well of deep commitment that made everything worthwhile. There seemed to be room in the universe for second chances and for that Ellie was grateful.

"I've been meaning to check this out." She followed him into the dark interior of the three-hundred-year-old church. Tombs of the longtime residents of the town lined the walls. He stood in front of the Andrewses' pew and walked around it to come to a tomb against the wall. It was Hannah's grave. Elaborate, it was decorated by a guilty father perhaps. He touched her name gently and was momentarily startled when somebody behind him cleared his throat.

"You're interested in Hannah Andrews?" the rector asked.

"My wife's family is related."

"He married her here, you know," the clergyman announced.

"What?" Ellie gasped. "Hannah Andrews was married?"

"Follow me." The rector took them into the back room where rows of leather-bound books lined the walls. They heard the children's giggles through the walls and smiled.

The rector's fingers danced down the rows of books and rested on a cracked column. "Aha, let me see..." He opened it and scanned the pages. "Here it is." He pointed an ink-stained finger at two names and a date. "'Hannah Andrews married John Wendover,' secretly, I may add," he said and looked up at them conspiratorially, "'on September 25, 1777.' Here is John's death. He was hung, as a traitor October first. She threw herself into the well, October second."

"They said her lover threw her into the well, because he couldn't have her."

The rector shook his head. "Her father told everyone that, because as a suicide, she would not have been allowed to be buried."

Paul continued, "On hallowed ground. Church rules. People who kill themselves can't be buried on church land. Do you know where John is?"

"However rich and powerful Geoffrey Andrews was, he was no match for the Wendovers. John Wendover has been in the tomb with her for years."

Paul reached into his pocket and pulled out Hannah's ring. In his other pocket, he had her diary. Handing it to the clergyman, he said, "I think these belong here."

The rector smiled and took the objects. "I believe they've been waiting for them." He placed them on the top of the tomb.

The wind sighed through the church, raising goose bumps. The sun peeked through the stained glass windows, leaving their faces filled with wonder.

Author's Note

Long Island was mostly pro-England or Loyalist during the Revolutionary War. After the Battle of Brooklyn, troops were quartered and stayed throughout most of the conflict. Historical plaques dot the island, naming places that became famous for housing high-ranking people involved in the war.

Stillwell Manor is a figment of my imagination as is the library, and many of the streets mentioned in the book.

St. John's Church is a beautiful white clapboard church in Cold Spring Harbor on Long Island. It sits atop a hill as described and has many tombs from the locals from the 1800s.

While the island stayed loyal to King George, the Townsend family of Oyster Bay became patriotic. Though their home, Raynham House, served as headquarters for the British army, the family remained ardent rebels. It is rumored that Lt. Col. John Graves Simcoe fell madly in love with the daughter of the house, Sally Townsend. In fact, the first known Valentine in America was found among her effects when she died a spinster at eighty-two.

It was also reported that Sally intercepted a message from Major John Andre regarding Benedict Arnold's surrender of West Point. Through her brother, they managed to get the message to General George Washington, causing Andre's capture. It is said that both the ghosts of Sally Townsend, as well as John Andre, haunt the house. But that's another story.

Another note about psychics. While Georgia Oaken is not a real person, the "session" is based on one I recently attended. Though the names and circumstances were different, the session ran similarly and was an enlightening experience.

About the Author

Born and raised on Long Island, Michael has always had a fascination with paranormal and ghostly tales. He earned a degree in English and an MBA, and he has worked various jobs before settling into being a full-time author. He currently resides on Long Island with his wife and children. *Stillwell* is his second novel.

michaelphillipcash@gmail.com

Made in the USA
Lexington, KY
04 November 2015